"You must have known I couldn't allow you to escape unscathed?"

"There is nothing you can do to prevent me from walking out of here."

"I want my daughter, Carly," he declared in a voice that was implacable, emotionless and totally without pity.

"Blackmail is a criminal offense!"

"I have stated my intention and given you a choice," he said harshly, and her eyes glittered with rage.

"I refuse to consider a mockery of a marriage, with a husband who divides his time between a wife and a mistress!"

"Your obsession with innuendo and supposition hasn't diminished," Stefano dismissed with deadly softness.

"Nor has my hatred of you!"

HELEN BIANCHIN, originally from New Zealand, met the man she would marry on a tobacco farm in Australia. Danilo, an Italian immigrant, spoke little English. Helen's Italian was nil. But communicate they did, and within eight weeks, Danilo found the words to ask Helen to marry him. With such romantic beginnings, it's a wonder that the author waited until after the birth of their third child to begin her prolific romance-writing career.

Books by Helen Bianchin

HARLEQUIN PRESENTS
1240—TOUCH THE FLAME
1383—THE TIGER'S LAIR
1423—THE STEFANOS MARRIAGE
1527—NO GENTLE SEDUCTION
1561—STORMFIRE
1601—RELUCTANT CAPTIVE

HARLEQUIN ROMANCE
2010—BEWILDERED HAVEN
2084—AVENGING ANGEL
2175—THE HILLS OF HOME
2387—MASTER OF ULURU

Don't miss any of our special offers. Write to us at the following address for information on our newest releases.

Harlequin Reader Service
U.S.: 3010 Walden Ave., P.O. Box 1325, Buffalo, NY 14269
Canadian: P.O. Box 609, Fort Erie, Ont. L2A 5X3

Helen Bianchin

PASSION'S MISTRESS

Harlequin Books

TORONTO • NEW YORK • LONDON
AMSTERDAM • PARIS • SYDNEY • HAMBURG
STOCKHOLM • ATHENS • TOKYO • MILAN
MADRID • WARSAW • BUDAPEST • AUCKLAND

ISBN 0-373-11704-3

PASSION'S MISTRESS

Copyright © 1994 by Helen Bianchin.

All rights reserved. Except for use in any review, the reproduction or utilization of this work in whole or in part in any form by any electronic, mechanical or other means, now known or hereafter invented, including xerography, photocopying and recording, or in any information storage or retrieval system, is forbidden without the written permission of the publisher, Harlequin Enterprises Limited, 225 Duncan Mill Road, Don Mills, Ontario, Canada M3B 3K9.

All characters in this book have no existence outside the imagination of the author and have no relation whatsoever to anyone bearing the same name or names. They are not even distantly inspired by any individual known or unknown to the author, and all incidents are pure invention.

This edition published by arrangement with Harlequin Enterprises B.V.

® and TM are trademarks of the publisher. Trademarks indicated with ® are registered in the United States Patent and Trademark Office, the Canadian Trade Marks Office and in other countries.

Printed in U.S.A.

CHAPTER ONE

IT WAS one of those beautiful southern hemispheric summer evenings with a soft balmy breeze drifting in from the sea.

An evening more suited to casual entertainment outdoors than a formal gathering, Carly mused as she stepped into a classically designed black gown and slid the zip in place. Beautifully cut, the style emphasised her slim curves and provided a perfect foil for her fine-textured skin.

A quick glance in the mirror revealed an attractive young woman of average height, whose natural attributes were enhanced by a glorious riot of auburn-streaked dark brown curls cascading halfway down her back.

The contrast was dramatic and far removed from the elegant chignon and classically tailored clothes she chose to wear to the office.

Indecision momentarily clouded her expression as she viewed her pale, delicately boned features. *Too* pale, she decided, and in a moment of utter recklessness she applied more blusher, then added another touch of eyeshadow to give extra emphasis to her eyes.

There, that would have to do, she decided as she viewed her image with critical appraisal, reflecting a trifle wryly that it was ages since she'd attended a social function—although tonight's soirée was entirely business, arranged for the express purpose

of affording a valuable new client introduction to
key personnel, and only her employer's insistence
had been instrumental in persuading her to join
other staff members at his house.

'All done,' she said lightly as she turned towards
the small pyjama-clad girl sitting cross-legged on
the bed: a beautiful child whose fragility tore at
Carly's maternal heartstrings and caused her to
curse silently the implicit necessity to attend tonight's party.

'You look pretty.' The voice held wistful admir-
ation, and a wealth of unreserved love shone from
wide, expressive dark eyes.

'Thank you,' Carly accepted gently as she leant
forward and trailed slightly shaky fingers down the
length of her daughter's dark, silky curls.

Tomorrow the waiting would be over. In a way,
it would be a relief to know the medical reason why
Ann-Marie's health had become so precarious in
the past few months. The round of referrals from
general practitioner to paediatrician, to one
specialist and then another, the seemingly endless
number of tests and X-rays had proven emotionally
and financially draining.

If Ann-Marie required the skills of a surgeon and
private hospital care . . .

Silent anguish gnawed at her stomach, then with
a concentrated effort Carly dampened her anxiety
and forced her wide, mobile mouth into a warm
smile as she clasped Ann-Marie's hand in her own.

'Sarah has the telephone number if she needs to
contact me,' she relayed gently as she led the way
towards the lounge.

Leaving Ann-Marie, even with someone as competent as Sarah, was a tremendous wrench. Especially tonight, when apprehension heightened her sense of guilt and warred violently with any need for divided loyalty. Yet her work was important, the money earned essential. Critical, she added silently.

Besides, Ann-Marie couldn't be in better hands than with Sarah, who, as a nursing sister at the Royal Children's Hospital, was well qualified to cope with any untoward eventuality.

'The dress is perfect.'

Carly smiled in silent acknowledgement of the warmly voiced compliment. 'It's kind of you to lend it to me.'

The attractive blonde rose from the sofa with unselfconscious grace. 'Your hair looks great. You should wear it like that more often.'

'Yes,' Ann-Marie agreed, and, tilting her head to one side, she viewed her mother with the solemn simplicity of the very young. 'It makes you look different.'

'Sophisticated,' Sarah added with a teasing laugh as she collected a book from the coffee-table. It was a popular children's story, with beautiful illustrations. 'Ann-Marie and I have some serious reading to do.'

Carly blessed Sarah's intuitive ability to distract Ann-Marie's attention—and her own, if only momentarily.

Their friendship went back seven years to the day they'd moved into neighbouring apartments—each fleeing her own home town for differing reasons, and each desperate for a new beginning.

'I won't be away any longer than I have to,' she assured quietly, then she gave Ann-Marie a hug, and quickly left.

In the lobby, Carly crossed to the lift and stabbed the call-button, hearing an answering electronic hum as the lift rose swiftly to the third floor, then just as swiftly transported her down to the basement.

The apartment block comprised three levels, and was one of several lining the northern suburban street, sharing a uniformity of pale brick, tiled roof, and basement car park, the only visual difference being a variation in the grassed verges and gardens, dependent on the generosity of any caring tenant who possessed both the time and inclination to beautify his or her immediate environment.

Carly unlocked her sedan, slid in behind the wheel and urged the aged Ford on to street level, taking the main arterial route leading into the city. It was almost seven-thirty, and unless there were any delays with traffic she should arrive at the requested time.

Clive Mathorpe owned an exclusive harbourside residence in Rose Bay, and a slight frown creased her forehead as she attempted to recall a previous occasion when her employer had organised a social event in his home for the benefit of a client—even the directorial scion of a vast entrepreneurial empire.

Acquiring Consolidated Enterprises had been quite a *coup*, for Mathorpe and Partners bore neither the size nor standing of any one of the three instantly recognisable internationally affiliated accounting firms.

Carly's speculation faded as she caught a glimpse of towering multi-level concrete and glass spires vying for supremacy in a city skyline, followed within minutes by an uninterrupted view of the unique architectural masterpiece of the Opera House.

It was a familiar scene she'd come to appreciate, for it was here in this city that she had developed a sense of self-achievement, together with an inner satisfaction at having strived hard against difficult odds and won. Not handsomely, she admitted a trifle wryly, aware of the leasing fee on her apartment and the loan on her car.

Negotiating inner-city evening traffic demanded total concentration, and Carly gave a silent sigh of relief when she reached Rose Bay.

Locating her employer's address presented no problem, and she slid the car to a halt outside an imposing set of wrought-iron gates.

Minutes later she took a curving path towards the main entrance, and within seconds of pressing the doorbell she was greeted by name and ushered indoors.

It was crazy suddenly to be stricken with an attack of nerves; mad to consider herself a social alien among people she knew and worked with.

Soft muted music vied with the chatter of variously toned voices, and Carly cast the large lounge and its occupants an idle sweeping glance. Without exception the men all wore black dinner-suits, white silk shirts and black bow-ties, while the women had each chosen stylish gowns in a concerted effort to impress.

Within minutes she was offered a drink, and she managed a slight smile as Bradley Williamson moved to her side. He was a pleasant man in his early thirties and considered to be one of Mathorpe and Partners' rising young executives.

His roving appraisal was brief, and his eyes assumed an appreciative sparkle as he met her steady gaze. 'Carly, you look sensational.'

'Bradley,' she acknowledged, then queried idly, 'Has Clive's honoured guest arrived yet?'

His voice took on an unaccustomed dryness. 'You're hoping he'll appear soon and let you off the figurative hook.'

It was a statement she didn't refute. 'Maybe he won't come,' she proffered absently, and caught Bradley's negative shake of the head.

'Doubtful. Mathorpe revealed that the director favours a personal touch in all his business dealings. "Involvement on every level" were his exact words.'

'Which explains why the company has achieved such success.'

Bradley spared her a quizzical smile that broadened his pleasant features into moderate attractiveness. 'Been doing your homework?'

Her answering response was without guile. 'Of course.' Figures, projections, past successes had been readily available. Yet mystery surrounded Consolidated Enterprises' top man, inviting intense speculation with regard to his identity.

'Such dedication,' he teased. 'The way you're heading, you'll be the first woman partner in the firm.'

'I very much doubt it.'

His interest quickened. 'You can't possibly be considering resigning in favour of working elsewhere.'

'No,' Carly disclaimed. 'I merely expressed the observation that Clive Mathorpe has tunnel vision, and, while an accountant of the feminine gender is quite acceptable in the workforce, taking one on as a partner is beyond his personal inclination.' A faint smile tugged the corners of her generously moulded mouth. 'Besides, I'm comfortable with things as they are.'

He absorbed her words and effected a philosophical shrug. 'Can I get you another drink?'

'Thank you. Something long, cool and mildly alcoholic.' She smiled at his expression, then added teasingly, 'Surprise me.'

Carly watched Bradley's departing back with an odd feeling of restlessness, aware of a time when her slightest need had been anticipated with unerring accuracy, almost as if the man in her life possessed an ability to see beyond the windows of her mind right to the very depths of her soul. Those were the days of love and laughter, when life itself had seemed as exotic and ebullient as the bubbles set free in a flute of the finest champagne.

Entrapped by introspection, Carly fought against the emergence of a vision so vivid, so shockingly compelling, that it was almost as if the image had manifested itself into reality.

Seven years hadn't dimmed her memory by the slightest degree. If anything the passage of those years had only served to magnify the qualities of a man she doubted she would ever be able to forget.

Their attraction had been instantaneous, a combustible force fired by electric fusion, and everything, everyone, from that moment on, had faded into insignificance. At twenty, she hadn't stood a chance against his devastating sexual alchemy, and within weeks he'd slipped a brilliant diamond on to her finger, charmed her widowed mother into planning an early wedding, and succeeded in sweeping Carly into the depths of passionate oblivion.

For the first three months of her marriage she had been blissfully, heavenly happy. Then the demands of her husband's business interests had begun to intrude into their personal life. Initially she hadn't queried the few occasions he rang to cancel dinner; nor had she thought to doubt that his overnight business trips were anything other than legitimate. Their reunions had always been filled with such a degree of sexual urgency that it never occurred to her that there could be anyone else.

Yet the rumours had begun, persistently connecting her husband with Angelica Agnelli. The two families had been linked together in various business interests for more than a generation, and Angelica, with qualifications in business management to her credit, held a seat on the board of directors of numerous companies.

Tall, slim, *soignée*, Angelica was the visual image of an assertive, high-powered businesswoman with her eye firmly set on the main chance. And that had included the man at the top of the directorial board. The fact that he had been legally and morally unavailable was considered of little or no consequence, his wife merely a minor obstacle that could easily be dismissed.

Carly's husband was possessed of an entrepreneurial flair that was the envy of his contemporaries, and his generosity to numerous charities was well known, thus ensuring his presence at prominent social events in and around Perth.

Carly reflected bitterly that it hadn't taken long for the gossip to take seed and germinate. Nor for the arguments to begin, and to continue unresolved until ultimately a devastating confrontation had finally supplied the will for her to escape.

Throughout her flight east she had been besieged by the machinations of her own imagination as it provided a litany of possible scenarios, and during those first few weeks in Sydney she'd lived on a knife-edge of nervous tension, fearful that her whereabouts might be discovered.

The bitter irony of having figuratively burned her bridges soon had become apparent with the knowledge she was pregnant.

The solution was something she'd chosen to face alone, and even in the depths of her own dilemma it had never occurred to her to consider abortion as the easy way out. Nor in those first few months of her pregnancy had she enlightened her widowed mother, and afterwards it was too late when emergency surgery resulted in her mother's death.

That initial year after Ann-Marie's birth had been difficult, caring for a child while juggling study and attempting a career. However, she'd managed...thanks to a private day-care centre and Sarah's help.

It was a source of pride that not only had she achieved success in her chosen field of accountancy, she'd also added a string of qualifications to her name that had earned respect from her peers.

'Sorry I took so long.'

Carly was brought sharply back to the present at the sound of Bradley's voice, and her lashes swept down to form a protective veil as she struggled to shut out the past.

'Your drink. I hope you like it.'

She accepted the glass with a slight smile, and murmured her thanks.

It was relief when several minutes later one of the firm's partners joined them and the conversation shifted entirely to business. A recent change in tax legislation had come into effect, and Carly entered into a lengthy debate with both men over the far-reaching implications on various of their clients' affairs.

Carly became so involved that at first she didn't notice a change in the background noise until a slight touch on her arm alerted her to examine the source of everyone's attention.

Clive Mathorpe's bulky frame was instantly recognisable. The man at his side stood at ease, his height and breadth a commanding entity. Even from this distance there was sufficient familiarity evident to send her heart thudding into an accelerated beat.

A dozen times over the past seven years she'd been shocked into immobility by the sight of a tall, broad-framed, dark-haired man, only to collapse with relief on discovering that the likeness was merely superficial.

Now, Carly stood perfectly still as logic vied with the possibility of coincidental chance, and even as she dismissed the latter there was a subtle shift in his stance so that his profile was revealed, eliminating any doubt as to his identity.

For one horrifying second Carly sensed the dark void of oblivion welling up and threatening to engulf her.

She couldn't, *dared not* faint. The humiliation would be too incredible and totally beyond conceivable explanation.

With conscious effort she willed herself to breathe slowly, deeply, in an attempt to retain some measure of composure as every single nerve-end went into a state of wild panic.

Stefano Alessi. Australian-born of Italian parents, he was a proven successor to his father's financial empire and a noted entrepreneur, having gained accolades and enjoyed essential prestige among his peers. In his late thirties, he was known to head vast multinational corporations, and owned residences in several European cities.

It was seven years since she'd last seen him. Seven years in which she'd endeavoured to forget the cataclysmic effect he'd had on her life.

Even now he had the power to liquefy her bones, and she watched with a sense of dreaded fascination as he glanced with seeming casualness round the room, almost as if an acutely developed sixth sense had somehow alerted him to her presence.

Carly mentally steeled herself for the moment of recognition, mesmerised by the sheer physical force of the man who had nurtured her innocent emotions and stoked them into a raging fire.

His facial features were just as dynamically arresting as she remembered, distinctive by their assemblage of broad-sculpted bone-structure, his wide-spaced, piercing grey eyes able to assess, dissect and categorise with definitive accuracy.

Dark brown, almost black hair moulded his head with well-groomed perfection, and he looked older—*harder*, she perceived, aware of the indomitable air of power evident that set him aside from every other man in the room.

She shivered, hating the way her body reacted to his presence, and there was nothing she could do to prevent the blood coursing through her veins as it brought all her senses tingling into vibrant life. Even her skin betrayed her, the soft surface hairs rising in silent recognition, attuned to a memory so intense, so incredibly acute, that she felt it must be clearly apparent to anyone who happened to look at her.

In seeming slow motion he captured her gaze, and the breath caught in her throat as his eyes clashed with hers for an infinitesimal second, searing with laser precision through every protective barrier to her soul, only to withdraw and continue an encompassing appraisal of the room's occupants.

'Our guest of honour is an attractive man, don't you think?'

Carly heard Bradley's voice as if from an immense distance, and she attempted a non-committal rejoinder that choked in her throat.

'I doubt there's a woman present who isn't wondering if he performs as well in the bedroom as he

does in the boardroom,' he assessed with wry
amusement.

All Carly wanted to do was escape the room, the
house. Yet even as she gathered her scattered wits
together she experienced a distinct feeling of dread
with the knowledge that any form of retreat was
impossible.

It became immediately apparent that Clive
Mathorpe intended to effect an introduction to key
personnel, and every passing second assumed the
magnitude of several minutes as the two men moved
slowly round the room.

Consequently, she was almost at screaming point
when Clive Mathorpe eventually reached her side.

'Bradley Williamson, one of my junior partners.'

The lines fanning out from Clive Mathorpe's
astute blue eyes deepened in silent appreciation of
Carly's fashion departure from studious employee.
'Carly Taylor, an extremely efficient young woman
who gives one hundred per cent to anything she
undertakes.' He paused, then added with a degree
of reverent emphasis, 'Stefano Alessi.'

It was a name which had gained much notice in
the business section of a variety of newspapers over
the past few months. Twice his photograph had
been emblazoned in the tabloid Press accompanied
by a journalistic report lauding the cementing of
yet another lucrative deal. Even in the starkness of
black and white newsprint, his portrayed persona
had emanated an electrifying magnetism that Carly
found difficult to dispel.

She held little doubt that the passage of seven
years had seen a marked escalation of his invest-
ment portfolio. On a personal level, she couldn'

help wondering whether Angelica Agnelli was still sharing his bed.

An ache started up in the region of her heart with a physicality so intense it became a tangible pain. Even now she could still hurt, and she drew on all her reserves of strength to present a cool, unaffected façade.

Cool grey eyes deliberately raked her slender frame, pausing imperceptibly on the slight fullness of her breasts before lifting to linger briefly on the generous curve of her mouth.

It was worse, much worse, than if he'd actually touched her. Equally mortifying was her body's instant recognition of the effect he had on all its sensual pleasure spots, and there was nothing she could do to still the betraying pulse at the edge of her throat as it quickened into a palpably visible beat.

Rage flared deep within, licking every nerve-fibre until it threatened to engulf her in overwhelming flame. How *dared* he subject her to such a sexist scrutiny? Almost as if she was an available conquest he was affording due contemplation.

Then his eyes met hers, and she almost died at the ruthlessness apparent, aware that his slight smile was a mere facsimile as he inclined his head in greeting.

'Miss Taylor.' His voice was a barely inflected drawl, each word given an imperceptible mocking emphasis.

'Mr Alessi,' Carly managed in polite response, although there was nothing she could do about the erratic beat of her heart in reaction to his proximity.

Something flared deep within her, a stirring that was entirely sexual—unwarranted and totally unwanted, yet there none the less—and it said much for her acquired measure of control that she managed to return his gaze with apparent equanimity.

His eyes darkened measurably, then without a further word he moved the necessary few steps to greet the next employee awaiting introduction.

Carly's mind reeled as several conflicting emotions warred in silent turmoil. Was his presence here tonight sheer coincidence, or did he have an ulterior motive?

She'd covered her tracks so well. She had even consulted a solicitor within days of arrival in Sydney, instructing that a letter be dispatched requesting any formalities to be handled by their individual legal representatives.

In seven years there had been no contact whatsoever.

It seemed incredibly ironic that Stefano should reappear at a time when she'd been forced to accept that he was the last ace in her pack should she have to raise more money for Ann-Marie's medical expenses.

Where her daughter's well-being was concerned there was no contest. Even it if meant sublimating her own personal reservations, and effecting a confrontation. His power and accumulated wealth could move figurative mountains, and if it was necessary she wouldn't hesitate to beg.

Carly caught the lower edge of her lip between two sharp teeth, then winced in silent pain as she unconsciously drew blood.

The desire to make some excuse and leave was strong. Yet only cowards cut and ran. This time she had to stay, even if the effort almost killed her.

Carly found each minute dragged interminably, and more than once her eyes strayed across the room to where Stefano Alessi stood conversing with Clive Mathorpe and two senior partners.

In his presence, all other men faded into insignificance. There was an exigent force apparent, which, combined with power and sexual magnetism, drew the attention of women like bees to a honeypot.

It was doubtful there was one female present whose pulse hadn't quickened at the sight of him, or whose imagination wasn't stirred by the thought of being able to captivate his interest.

Carly waited ten minutes after Stefano left before she crossed the room to exchange a few polite pleasantries with Clive Mathorpe and his wife, then she slipped quietly from the house and walked quickly down the driveway to her car.

Safely behind the wheel, she activated the ignition and eased the car forward. A quick glance at the illuminated dashboard revealed it was nine-thirty. One hour, she reflected with disbelief. For some reason it had seemed half a lifetime.

Stefano Alessi's disturbing image rose up to taunt her, and she shivered despite the evening's warmth. He represented everything she had come to loathe in a man.

For one brief milli-second she closed her eyes, then opened them to issue a silent prayer that fate wouldn't be so unkind as to throw her beneath his path again.

It was a relief to reach the sanctuary of her apartment building, and after garaging the car she rode the lift to the third floor.

'Hi,' Sarah greeted quietly as Carly entered the lounge. 'Ann-Marie's fine. How was the evening?'

I met Ann-Marie's father, she longed to confide.

Yet the words stayed locked in her throat, and she managed to relay an informative account as they shared coffee together, then when Sarah left she checked Ann-Marie before entering her own bedroom, where she mechanically removed her make-up and undressed ready for bed.

Sleep had never seemed more distant, and she tossed restlessly from one side to the other in a bid to dispel a flood of returning memories.

Haunting, invasive, they refused to be denied as one by one she began to recall the angry words she'd exchanged in bitter argument with a man she'd chosen to condemn.

CHAPTER TWO

CARLY slept badly, haunted by numerous dream sequences that tore at her subconscious mind with such vivid clarity that she woke shaking, shattered by their stark reality.

A warning, perhaps? Or simply the manifestation of a fear so real that it threatened to consume her?

Tossing aside the covers, she resolutely went through the motions entailed in her early morning weekday routine, listening to Ann-Marie's excited chatter over breakfast as she recounted events from the previous evening.

When pressed to reveal just how *her* evening had turned out, Carly brushed it off lightly with a smile and a brief but satisfactory description.

It was eight-thirty when Carly deposited Ann-Marie outside the school gates, and almost nine when she entered the reception area of Mathorpe and Partners.

There were several files on her desk demanding attention, and she worked steadily, methodically checking figures with determined dedication until mid-morning when she reached for the phone and punched out a series of digits.

The specialist's receptionist was extremely polite, but firm. Ann-Marie's results could not be given over the phone. An appointment had been set aside this afternoon for four o'clock.

It sounded ominous, and Carly's voice shook as she confirmed the time.

The remainder of the day was a blur as anxiety played havoc with her nervous system, and in the specialist's consulting-rooms it was all she could do to contain it.

Consequently, it was almost an anticlimax when she was shown into his office, and as soon as she was comfortably seated he leaned back in his chair, his expression mirroring a degree of sympathetic understanding.

'Ann-Marie has a tumour derived from the supporting tissue of the nerve-cells,' he informed her quietly. 'The astrocytoma varies widely in malignancy and rate of growth. Surgery is essential, and I recommend it be carried out as soon as possible.'

Carly's features froze with shock at the professionally spoken words, and her mind immediately went into overdrive with a host of implications, the foremost of which was *money*.

'I can refer you to a neuro-surgeon, someone I consider to be the best in his field.' His practised pause held a silent query. 'I'll have my nurse arrange an appointment, shall I?'

The public hospital system was excellent, but the waiting list for elective surgery was long. Too long to gamble with her daughter's life. Carly didn't hesitate. 'Please.'

It took only minutes for the appointment to be confirmed; a few more to exchange pleasantries before the receptionist ushered Carly from his rooms.

She walked in a daze to her car, then slid in behind the wheel. A sick feeling of despair welled up inside as innate fear overruled rational thought, for no matter how hard she tried it was impossible to dispel the terrible image of Ann-Marie lying still and helpless in an operating theatre, her life reliant on the skill of a surgeon's scalpel.

It will be all right, Carly determined as she switched on the ignition, then eased her car on to the street. One way or another, she'd make sure of it.

The flow of traffic was swift, and on a few occasions it took two light changes to clear an intersection. Taxis were in demand, their drivers competent as they manoeuvred their vehicles from one lane to another, ready to take the first opportunity ahead of city commuters.

The cars in front began to slow, and Carly eased her sedan to a halt. Almost absently her gaze shifted slightly to the right, drawn as if by some elusive magnet to a top-of-the-range black Mercedes that had pulled up beside her in the adjacent lane.

Her eyes grazed towards the driver in idle, almost speculative curiosity, only to have them widen in dawning horror as she recognised the sculpted male features of none other than Stefano Alessi behind the wheel.

Her initial reaction was to look away, except she hesitated too long, and in seeming slow motion she saw him turn towards her.

With a sense of fatalism she saw his strong features harden, and she almost died beneath the intensity of his gaze.

Then a horn blast provided a startling intrusion, and Carly forced her attention to the slow-moving traffic directly ahead. In her hurry she crashed the gears and let the clutch out too quickly for her aged sedan's liking, causing it to stall in retaliatory protest.

Damn. The curse fell silently from her lips, and she twisted the ignition key, offering soothing words in the hope that the engine would fire.

An audible protest sounded from immediately behind, quickly followed by another, then a surge of power shook the small sedan and she eased it forward, picking up speed as she joined the river of cars vacating the city.

It wasn't until she'd cleared the intersection that she realised how tight a grip she retained on the wheel. A light film of moisture beaded her upper lip in visible evidence of her inner tension, and she forced herself to relax, angry that the mere sight of a man she professed to hate could affect her so deeply.

It took almost an hour to reach Manly, yet it felt as if she'd been battling traffic for twice that long by the time she garaged the car.

Upstairs, Sarah opened the door, her eyes softening with concern at the sight of Carly's pale features.

'Sarah helped me draw some pictures.'

Carly leant forward and hugged her daughter close. Her eyes were suspiciously damp as Ann-Marie's small arms fastened round her neck in loving reciprocation.

'I'll make coffee,' Sarah suggested, and Carly shot her friend a regretful smile.

'I can't stay.' Her eyes assumed a haunting vulnerability. 'I'll ring you.' She paused, then attempted a shaky smile. 'After eight?'

Entering her own apartment, Carly moved through to the kitchen and prepared their evening meal, then when the dishes had been dealt with she organised Ann-Marie's bath, made the little girl a hot milky drink, then tucked her into bed.

It was early, and she crossed to the phone to dial directory service, praying they could supply the number she needed.

Minutes later she learned there was no listing for Stefano Alessi, and the only number available was ex-directory. *Damn*.

Carly queried Consolidated Enterprises, and was given two numbers, neither of which responded at this hour of the night. There was no after-hours number listed, nor anything connected to a mobile net.

Carly cursed softly beneath her breath. She had no recourse but to wait until tomorrow. Unless she rang Clive Mathorpe at home and asked for his coveted client's private telephone number.

Even as the thought occurred, it was instantly dismissed. What could she offer as the reason for such an unorthodox request? Her esteemed boss would probably suffer an instant apoplectic attack if she were to say, 'Oh, by the way, Clive, I forgot to mention that Stefano Alessi is my estranged husband.'

Tomorrow, she determined with grim purpose. Even if she had to utilise devious means to obtain her objective.

A leisurely shower did little to soothe her fractured nerves, nor did an attempt to view television.

Long after she'd switched off the bedside lamp Stefano's image rose to taunt her, and even in dreams he refused to disappear, her subconscious mind forcing recognition of his existence, so that in consequence she spent another restless night fighting off several demons in numerous guises.

The next morning Carly dropped Ann-Marie at school then drove into the city, and on reaching her office she quietly closed her door so that she could make the necessary phone call in private.

It was crazy, but her nerves felt as if they were shredding to pieces as she waited for the call to connect, and only Ann-Marie's plight provided the courage needed to overcome the instinctive desire to replace the receiver.

Several minutes later, however, she had to concede that Stefano was virtually inaccessible to anyone but a chosen few. The majority were requested to supply verbal credentials and leave a contact telephone number.

The thought of waiting all day for him to return the call, even supposing he chose to, brought her out in a cold sweat. There was only one method left open to her whereby she retained some small measure of power, and she used it mercilessly.

'Stefano Alessi,' she directed coolly as soon as the receptionist answered, and, hardly giving the girl a chance to draw breath, she informed her, 'Tell his secretary his wife is on the line.' That should bring some response.

It did, and Carly derived some satisfaction from the girl's barely audible surprise. Within seconds the call was transferred, and another female voice requested verification.

Stefano's personal staff were hand-picked to handle any eventuality with unruffled calm—and even a call from someone purporting to be the director's wife failed to faze his secretary in the slightest.

'Mr Alessi isn't in the office. Can I have him call you?'

Damn. She could hardly ask for his mobile number, for it would automatically be assumed that she already had it. 'What time do you expect him in?'

'This afternoon. He has an appointment at three, followed by another at four.'

Assertiveness was the key, and Carly didn't hesitate. 'Thank you. I'll be there at four-thirty.' She hung up, then quickly made two further calls—one to Sarah asking if she could collect Ann-Marie from school, and another to Ann-Marie's teacher confirming the change in routine.

The day loomed ahead, once again without benefit of a lunch-hour, and Carly worked diligently in an effort to recoup lost time.

At precisely four-fifteen Carly entered the lobby of a towering glass-faced edifice housing the offices of Consolidated Enterprises, stabbed the call-button to summon one of four lifts, then when it arrived stepped into the cubicle and pressed the designated disk.

The nerves she had striven to keep at bay surfaced with painful intensity, and she mentally steeled herself for the moment she had to walk into Reception and identify herself.

By now Stefano's secretary would have informed him of her call. What if he refused to see her?

Positive, think *positive*, an inner voice urged.

The lift paused, the doors opened, and Carly had little option but to step into the luxuriously appointed foyer.

Reception lay through a set of wide glass doors, and, acting a part, she stepped forward and gave her name. Her eyes were clear and level, and her smile projected just the right degree of assurance.

The receptionist's reaction was polite, her greeting civil, and it was impossible for Carly to tell anything from her expression as she lifted a handset and spoke quietly into the receiver.

'Mr Alessi is still in conference,' the receptionist relayed. 'His secretary will escort you to his private lounge where you can wait in comfort.'

At least she'd passed the first stage, Carly sighed with silent relief as she followed an elegantly attired woman to a room whose interior design employed a mix of soft creams, beige and camel, offset by opulently cushioned sofas in plush chocolate-brown.

There were several current glossy magazines to attract her interest, an excellent view of the inner city if she chose to observe it through the wide expanse of plate-glass window. Even television, if she were so inclined, and a well-stocked drinks cabinet, which Carly found tempting—except that even the mildest measure of alcohol on an empty stomach would probably have the opposite effect on her nerves.

Coffee would be wonderful, and her hand hovered over the telephone console, only to return seconds later to her side. What if the connection went straight through to Stefano's office, instead of to his secretary?

Minutes passed, and she began to wonder if he wasn't playing some diabolical game.

Dear lord, he must know how difficult it was for her to approach him. Surely she'd suffered enough, without this latest insult?

The thought of seeing him again, alone, without benefit of others present to diffuse the devastating effect on her senses, made her feel ill.

Her stomach began to clench in painful spasms, and a cold sweat broke over her skin.

What was taking him so long? A quick glance at her watch determined that ten minutes had passed. How much longer before he deigned to make an appearance?

At that precise moment the door opened, and Carly's eyes flew to the tall masculine frame outlined in the aperture.

Unbidden, she rose to her feet, and her heart gave a sudden jolt, disturbed beyond measure by the lick of flame that swept through her veins. It was mad, utterly crazy that he could still have this effect, and she forced herself to breathe slowly in an attempt to slow the rapid beat of her pulse.

Attired in a dark grey business suit, blue silk shirt and tie, he appeared even more formidable than she'd expected, his height an intimidating factor as he entered the room.

The door closed behind him with a faint decisive snap, and for one electrifying second she felt trapped. Imprisoned, she amended, verging towards silent hysteria as her eyes lifted towards his in a gesture of contrived courage.

His harshly assembled features bore an inscrutability that was disquieting, and she viewed him warily as he crossed to stand within touching distance.

He embodied a dramatic mesh of blatant masculinity and elemental ruthlessness, his stance that of a superior jungle cat about to stalk a vulnerable prey, assessing the moment he would choose to pounce and kill.

Dammit, she derided silently. She was being too fanciful for words! A tiny voice taunted that he had no need for violence when he possessed the ability verbally to reduce even the most worthy opponent to a state of mute insecurity in seconds.

The silence between them was so acute that Carly was almost afraid to breathe, and she became intensely conscious of the measured rise and fall of her breasts, the painful beat of her heart as it seemed to leap through her ribcage. Her eyes widened fractionally as he thrust a hand into his trouser pocket with an indolent gesture, and she tilted her head, forcing herself to retain his gaze.

'Shall we dispense with polite inanities and go straight to the reason why you're here?' Stefano queried hardily.

There was an element of tensile steel beneath the sophisticated veneer, a sense of purpose that was daunting. She was aware of an elevated nervous tension, and it took every ounce of courage to speak calmly. 'I wasn't sure you'd see me.'

The eyes that speared hers were deliberately cool, and an icy chill feathered across the surface of her skin.

'Curiosity, perhaps?' His voice was a hateful drawl, and her eyes gleamed with latent anger, their depths flecked with tawny gold.

She wanted to *hit* him, to disturb his tightly held control. Yet such an action was impossible, for she couldn't afford to indulge in a display of temper. She needed him—or, more importantly, Ann-Marie needed the sort of help his money could bring.

'Coffee?'

She was tempted to refuse, and for a moment she almost did, then she inclined her head in silent acquiescence. 'Please.'

Dark grey eyes raked her slim form, then returned to stab her pale features with relentless scrutiny. Without a word he crossed to the telephone console and lifted the handset, then issued a request for coffee and sandwiches before turning back to face her.

His expression became chillingly cynical, assuming an inscrutability that reflected inflexible strength of will. 'How much, Carly?'

Her head lifted of its own volition, her eyes wide and clear as she fought to utter a civil response.

One eyebrow slanted in a gesture of deliberate mockery. 'I gather that is why you're here?'

She had already calculated the cost and added a fraction more in case of emergency. Now she doubled it. 'Twenty thousand dollars.'

He directed her a swift calculated appraisal, and when he spoke his voice was dangerously soft. 'That's expensive elective surgery.'

Carly's eyes widened into huge pools of incredulity as comprehension dawned, and for one brief second her eyes filled with incredible pain. Then a surge of anger rose to the surface, palpable, inimical, and beyond control.

Without conscious thought she reached for the nearest object at hand, uncaring of the injury she could inflict or any damage she might cause.

Stefano shifted slightly, and the rock-crystal ashtray missed its target by inches and crashed into a framed print positioned on the wall directly behind his shoulder.

The sound was explosive, and in seeming slow motion Carly saw the glass shatter, the framed print spring from its fixed hook and fall to the carpet. The ashtray followed its path, intact, to bounce and roll drunkenly to a halt in the centre of the room.

Time became a suspended entity, the silence so intense that she could hear the ragged measure of her breathing and feel the pounding beat of her heart.

She didn't move, *couldn't*, for the muscles activating each limb appeared suspended and beyond any direction from her brain.

It was impossible to gauge his reaction, for the only visible sign of anger apparent was revealed in the hard line of his jaw, the icy chill evident in the storm-grey darkness of his eyes.

The strident ring of the phone made her jump, its shrill sound diffusing the electric tension, and Carly watched in mesmerised fascination as Stefano crossed to the console and picked up the handset.

He listened for a few seconds, then spoke reassuringly to whoever was on the other end of the line.

More than anything, she wanted to storm out of the room, the building, *his life*. Yet she couldn't. Not yet.

Stefano slowly replaced the receiver, then he straightened, his expression an inscrutable mask.

'So,' he intoned silkily. 'Am I to assume from that emotive reaction that you aren't carrying the seed of another man's child, and are therefore not in need of an abortion?'

I carried yours, she longed to cry out. With determined effort she attempted to gather together the threads of her shattered nerves. 'Don't presume to judge me by the numerous women you bed,' she retorted in an oddly taut voice.

His eyes darkened until they resembled shards of obsidian slate. 'You have no foundation on which to base such an accusation.'

Carly closed her eyes, then slowly opened them again. 'It goes beyond my credulity to imagine you've remained celibate for seven years.' *As I have*, she added silently.

'You're here to put me on trial for supposed sexual misdemeanours during the years of our enforced separation?'

His voice was a hatefully musing drawl that made her palms itch with the need to resort to a display of physical anger.

'If you could sleep with Angelica during our marriage, I can't even *begin* to imagine what you might have done after I left!' Carly hurled with the pent-up bitterness of *years*.

There was a curious bleakness apparent, then his features assumed an expressionless mask as he cast his watch a deliberate glance. 'State your case, Carly,' he inclined with chilling disregard. 'In nine minutes I have an appointment with a valued colleague.'

It was hardly propitious to her cause continually to thwart him, and her chin tilted fractionally as she held his gaze. 'I already thought I had.'

'Knowing how much you despise me,' Stefano drawled softly, 'I can only be intrigued by the degree of desperation that forces you to confront me with a request for money.'

Her eyes were remarkably steady, and she did her best to keep the intense emotion from her voice. 'Someone I care for very much needs an operation,' she said quietly. It was true, even if it was truth by partial omission. 'Specialist care, a private hospital.'

One eyebrow lifted with mocking cynicism. 'A man?'

She curled her fingers into a tight ball and thrust her hands behind her back. 'No,' she denied in a curiously flat voice.

'Then who, Carly?' he queried silkily. His eyes raked hers, compelling, inexorable, and inescapable.

'A child.'

'Am I permitted to know *whose* child?'

He wouldn't give in until she presented him with all the details, and she suddenly hated him, with an intensity that was vaguely shocking, for all the pain, the anger and the futility, for having dared, herself, to love him unreservedly, only to have that love thrown back in her face.

Seven years ago she'd hurled one accusation after another at the man who had steadfastly refused to confirm, deny or explain his actions. As a result, she'd frequently given vent to angry recrimination which rarely succeeded in provoking his retaliation.

Except once. Then he'd castigated her as the child
he considered her to be, and when she'd hit him
he'd unceremoniously hauled her back into their
bed and subjected her to a lesson she was never
likely to forget.

The following morning she'd packed a bag, and
driven steadily east until hunger and exhaustion had
forced her to stop. Then she'd rung her mother,
offered the briefest of explanations and assured her
she'd be in touch.

That had been the last personal contact she'd had
with the man she had married. Until now.

'My daughter,' she enlightened starkly, and
watched his features reassemble, the broad facial
bones seeming more pronounced, the jaw clearly
defined beneath the taut musculature bonding fibre
to bone. The composite picture portrayed a harsh
ruthlessness she found infinitely frightening.

'I suggest,' he began in a voice pitched so low
that it sounded like silk being razed by steel, 'you
contact the child's father.'

Carly visibly shivered. His icy anger was almost
a tangible entity, cooling the room, and there was
a finality in his words, an inexorability she knew
she'd never be able to circumvent unless she told
the absolute truth—*now*.

'Ann-Marie was born exactly seven months and
three weeks after I left Perth.' There were papers
in her bag. A birth certificate, blood-group rec-
ords—hers, Ann-Marie's, a copy of *his*. Photos.
Several of them, showing Ann-Marie as a babe in
arms, a toddler, then on each consecutive birthday,
all showing an acute similarity to the man who had

fathered her: the same colouring, dark, thick, silky hair, and grey eyes.

Carly retrieved them, thrusting one after the other into Stefano's hands as irrefutable proof. 'She's your daughter, Stefano. *Yours*.'

The atmosphere in the lounge was so highly charged that Carly almost expected it to ignite into incendiary flame.

His expression was impossible to read, and as the seconds dragged silently by she felt like screaming—anything to get some reaction.

'Tell me,' Stefano began in a voice that was satin-smooth and dangerous, 'was I to be forever kept in ignorance of her existence?'

Oh, dear lord, how could she answer that? Should she even dare, when she wasn't sure of the answer herself? 'Maybe when she was older I would have offered her the opportunity to get in touch with you,' she admitted with hesitant honesty.

'*Grazie*.' His voice was as chilling as an ice floe in an arctic wasteland. 'And how, precisely, did you intend to achieve that? By having her turn up on my doorstep, ten, fifteen years from now, with a briefly penned note of explanation in her hand?'

He was furiously angry; the whiplash of his words tore at her defences, ripping them to shreds. 'Damn you,' he swore softly. 'Damn you to hell.'

He looked capable of anything, and she took an involuntary step backwards from the sheer force-field of his rage. 'Right at this moment, it would give me the utmost pleasure to wring your slender neck.' He appeared to rein in his temper with visible effort. 'What surgical procedure?' he demanded grimly. 'What's wrong with her?'

With a voice that shook slightly she relayed the details, watching with detached fascination as he scrawled a series of letters and numbers with firm, swift strokes on to a notepad.

'*Your* address and telephone number.' The underlying threat of anger was almost a palpable force. She could sense it, almost *feel* its intensity, and she felt impossibly afraid.

It took considerable effort to maintain an aura of calm, but she managed it. 'Your assurance that Ann-Marie's medical expenses will be met is all that's necessary.'

His eyes caught hers and held them captive, and she shivered at the ruthlessness apparent in their depths. 'You can't believe I'll hand over a cheque and let you walk out of here?' he said with deadly softness, and a cold hand suddenly clutched at her heart and squeezed hard.

'I'll make every attempt to pay you back,' Carly ventured stiffly, and saw his eyes harden.

'I intend that you shall.' His voice was velvet-encased steel, and caused the blood in her veins to chill.

A knock at the door provided an unexpected intrusion, and Carly cast him a startled glance as his secretary entered the room and placed a laden tray down on to the coffee-table. It said much for the secretary's demeanour that she gave no visible indication of having seen the deposed picture frame or the glass that lay scattered on the carpet.

Carly watched the woman's movements as she poured aromatic coffee from a steaming pot into two cups and removed clear plastic film from a plate of delectable sandwiches.

'Contact Bryan Thorpe, Renate,' Stefano instructed smoothly. 'Extend my apologies and reschedule our meeting for Monday.'

Renate didn't blink. 'Yes, of course.' She straightened from her task, her smile practised and polite as she turned and left the room.

Carly eyed the sandwiches with longing, aware that the last meal she'd eaten was breakfast. The coffee was tempting, and she lifted the cup to her lips with both hands, took a savouring sip, then shakily replaced it down on to the saucer.

The need to escape this room was almost as imperative as her desire to escape the man who occupied it, for despite her resolve his presence had an alarming effect on her equilibrium, stirring alive an entire gamut of emotions, the foremost of which was fear. The feeling was so intense that all her senses seemed elevated, heightened to a degree where she felt her entire body was a finely tuned instrument awaiting the maestro's touch. Which was crazy—*insane*.

'There's no need to cancel your appointment,' she told him with more courage than she felt, and she collected her bag and slid the strap over one shoulder in a silent indication of her intention to leave.

'Where do you think you're going?' Stefano said in a deadly soft voice, and she looked at him carefully, aware of the aura of strength, the indomitable power apparent, and experienced a stirring of alarm.

'Home.'

'I intend to see her.'

The words threw her off balance, and she went suddenly still. 'No,' she denied, stricken by the image of father and daughter meeting for the first time, the effect it would have on Ann-Marie. 'I don't want the disruption your presence will have on her life,' she offered shakily.

'Or yours,' he declared with uncanny perception. His eyes were hard, his expression inexorable. 'Yet you must have known that once I was aware of the facts there could be no way I'd allow you to escape unscathed?'

A shiver shook her slim frame; she was all too aware that she was dealing with a man whose power was both extensive and far-reaching. Only a fool would underestimate him, and right now he looked as if he'd like to shake her until she begged for mercy.

'There is nothing you can do to prevent me from walking out of here,' she said stiltedly.

'I want my daughter, Carly,' he declared in a voice that was implacable, emotionless, and totally without pity. 'Either we effect a reconciliation and resume our marriage, or I'll seek legal custody through court action. The decision is yours.'

A well of anger rose to the surface at his temerity. 'You have no right,' Carly retaliated fiercely. 'No——'

'You have until tomorrow to make up your mind.' He stroked a series of digits on to paper, tore it from its block, and handed it to her. 'You can reach me on this number.'

'Blackmail is a criminal offence!'

'I have stated my intention and given you a choice,' he said hardly, and her eyes glittered with rage.

'I refuse to consider a mockery of a marriage, with a husband who divides his time between a wife and a mistress!'

His eyes narrowed, and Carly met his gaze with fearless disregard. 'Don't bother attempting to deny it,' she advised with deep-seated bitterness. 'There was a succession of so-called friends and social acquaintances who took delight in ensuring I heard the latest gossip. One, in particular, had access to a Press-clipping service, and never failed to ensure that I received conclusive proof of your infidelity.'

'Your obsession with innuendo and supposition hasn't diminished,' Stefano dismissed with deadly softness.

'Nor has my hatred of you!'

His smile was a mere facsimile, and she was held immobile by the dangerous glitter in his eyes, the peculiar stillness of his stance. 'It says something for your maternal devotion that you managed to overcome it sufficiently to confront me.'

Angry, futile tears diminished her vision, and she blinked furiously to dispel them. 'Only because there was no other option!'

Without a word she turned and walked to the door, uncaring whether he attempted to stop her or not.

He didn't move, and she walked down the carpeted hallway to Reception, her head held high, pride forcing a faint smile as she inclined a slight nod to the girl manning the switchboard before sweeping out to the foyer.

A lift arrived within seconds of being summoned, and it wasn't until she reached ground level that reaction began to set in.

CHAPTER THREE

IT TOOK an hour for Carly to reach Manly, and she uttered a silent prayer of thanks to whoever watched over her as she traversed the car-choked arterial roads leading north from the city. Concentration was essential, and her own was in such a state of serious disarray that it was a minor miracle her sedan survived the drive intact.

Sarah answered the door at once, and Carly cast her a grateful glance as she entered her friend's apartment.

'Thanks for collecting Ann-Marie. I got held up, and the traffic slowed to a complete halt in places.'

'Sarah read me a story, and we watched television. I've already had my bath,' Ann-Marie informed her as she ran into her mother's outstretched arms.

Carly hugged the small body close, and felt the onset of emotion-packed tears. For more than six years she'd fought tooth and nail to support them both without any outside financial assistance. Soon that would change, and she wasn't sure she'd ever be ready for the upheaval Stefano Alessi would cause in their lives.

'Would you like some coffee?' Sarah queried. 'I'll put the kettle on.'

Carly shot her friend a distracted smile. 'Why not come over and share our meal?' It was the least she could do, and besides, it would be lovely to have company. Then she would have less time alone in which to think.

Sarah looked suitably regretful. 'I'd love to, but I'm going out tonight.'

Carly glimpsed the indecision apparent, the pensive brooding evident in Sarah's lovely blue eyes.

'I take it this isn't the usual casual meal shared with a female friend?' she queried slowly. 'Who's the lucky man?'

'A doctor who performed emergency surgery several months ago while I was on night duty. He's recently moved south from Cairns. We ran into each other a few days later, in the supermarket of all places, and we chatted. Then I saw him again at the hospital.' She paused, and effected a faint shrugging gesture. 'He's . . .' She paused, searching for the right words. 'Easy to talk to, I guess. Last week he asked me out to dinner.' Her eyes clouded, then deepened to cerulean blue. 'I said yes at the time, but now I'm not so sure.'

Aware that Sarah's disastrous first marriage and subsequent messy divorce had left her with a strong dislike and distrust of men, almost to the point where she refused to have anything to do with them other than in a professional capacity, Carly could only wonder at the man who had managed to break through her friend's defences.

'I'm delighted for you,' she declared with genuine sincerity.

'I'm terrified for me,' Sarah acknowledged wryly as she filled both mugs with boiling water.

The aroma of instant coffee was no substitute for the real thing, but the hot, sweet brew had a necessary reviving effect and Carly sipped the contents of her mug with appreciative satisfaction.

'What time is he picking you up?'

'Seven.' An entire gamut of emotions chased fleetingly across Sarah's attractive features. 'I'm going to ring him and cancel.'

If he was at all intuitive, he would have deliberately left his answering machine off with just this possibility in mind, Carly reflected as Sarah crossed to the telephone and punched out the requisite digits, only to listen and replace the receiver.

'Damn. Now what am I going to do?'

Carly viewed her with twinkling solemnity. 'Go out with him.'

'I can't. I'm nuts,' Sarah wailed. '*Nuts.*' Her expression assumed a sudden fierceness. 'If the situation were reversed, would *you* go out with another man?'

Her heart lurched, then settled into an accelerated beat in the knowledge that she would soon be inextricably involved with someone she'd sworn never to have anything to do with again, coerced by a set of circumstances that denied any freedom of choice. Yet her academic mind demanded independent legal verification of Stefano's threat of custody, even as logic reasoned that in a court of law the odds would be heavily stacked against Stefano being denied access to his daughter. Tomorrow was Saturday, but there was a friend she could contact outside office hours who would relay the vital information she needed.

'Carly?'

She proffered a faint smile in silent apology and shook her head. 'Not all men are made from the same mould as our respective first husbands,' she managed, evading Sarah's close scrutiny as she lifted the mug to her lips and sipped from it.

'When he arrives, I'll tell him I've changed my mind,' Sarah declared, and, placing a light hand on Carly's arm, she queried softly, 'Are you OK?'

There was no time for confidences, and Carly wasn't sure she was ready to share Stefano's ultimatum with anyone. 'I'm fine,' she assured quietly as she deliberately forced a slight smile. 'Let me give Ann-Marie dinner, then I'll come and help with your hair.'

Sarah shot her a dark musing glance. 'He's seen me in denim shorts, a T-shirt, trainers, and no make-up.' Her expression became faintly speculative as she took in the paleness of Carly's features, the edge of tension apparent. 'Give me twenty minutes to shower and change.'

Once in her own apartment, it took only a few minutes to heat the casserole she'd prepared the previous evening, and although Ann-Marie ate well Carly mechanically forked small portions from her plate with little real appetite.

Afterwards Ann-Marie proved an interested spectator as Carly used hot rollers to good effect on Sarah's hair.

'Why do I feel as nervous as a teenager about to go on a first date?' Sarah queried with wry disbelief. 'No, don't answer that.'

'All done,' Carly announced minutes later as she stepped back a pace to view the style she'd effected with critical favour. 'You look really great,' she assured her gently, her eyes softening with genuine feeling for her friend's state of panic. 'Are you

going to tell me his name?' she prompted with a
faintly teasing smile.

'James Hensley,' Sarah revealed. 'Surgeon, late
thirties, widower, one son. He's slightly aloof and
distinguished, yet warm and easy to talk to, if that
makes sense.' Indecision, doubt and anxiety clouded
her attractive features. A deprecatory laugh merged
with an audible groan of despair. 'Why am I doing
this to myself? I don't *need* the emotional
aggravation!'

The intercom buzzed, and Carly reached out and
caught hold of Ann-Marie's hand. 'Have a really
fantastic time,' she bade Sarah gently. 'We'll let
ourselves out.'

It was after eight before Ann-Marie fell asleep,
and Carly gently closed the storybook, then gazed
at her daughter's classic features in repose. She
looked so small, so fragile. Far too young to have
to undergo extensive surgery. Her beautiful
hair——

A lump rose in Carly's throat, a painful constric-
tion she had difficulty in swallowing. It wasn't fair.
Life wasn't fair. Dammit, she wouldn't cry. Tears
were for the weak, and she had to be strong. For
both of them. At least her daughter would have the
best medical attention money could buy, she consoled herself fiercely.

Carly remained seated in the chair beside Ann-
Marie's bed for a long time before she stirred herself
sufficiently to leave the room, and after carefully
closing the door she crossed the lounge to the
phone.

Twenty minutes later she slowly replaced the receiver. With a sinking heart she attempted to come

to terms with the fact that any claim for custody
by Stefano could succeed. Sole custody was not a
consideration unless he could prove indisputably
that Carly was an unfit mother. However, he could
insist on joint custody—alternate weekends, half
of each school holiday—and be granted any
reasonable request for access.

On that premise, Carly was sufficiently intelligent to be aware of what would happen if she con-
tested his claim in a court of law, or what emphasis
his lawyer would place on her decision to leave
Stefano in ignorance of Ann-Marie's existence.

She closed her eyes, almost able to hear the
damning words uttered with appropriate dramatic
inflexion. The moral issue would be played out with
stunning effect. With the added weight of Stefano's
wealth, she wouldn't stand a chance of him being
refused custody.

Without conscious thought she sank into a nearby
chair in despair. Dear God, she agonised shakily.
How could she do that to her daughter? Ann-Marie
would be pulled and pushed between two people
who no longer had anything in common, torn by
divided loyalties, and unsure whether either parent's
affection was motivated by genuine love or a desire
to hurt the other.

In years to come Ann-Marie would understand
and comprehend the truth of her parents' relationship. But what damage would be done between now
and then? It didn't bear thinking about.

There was really no choice. None at all.

Impossibly restless, she flung herself into completing a punishing few hours of housework, followed by a stint of ironing. At least it provided an

outlet for her nervous tension, and she tumbled wearily into bed to toss and turn far into the early hours of the morning.

'You look—terrible,' Sarah declared with concern as Carly answered the door shortly after eleven. 'Is Ann-Marie OK?'

'She's fine,' Carly responded with a faint smile, then winced at the increasing pain in her head. 'She's dressing her doll in the bedroom and deciding what she should wear to Susy's party this afternoon. Come on in, we'll have some coffee.'

'I'll make the coffee, *and* get you something for that headache,' Sarah insisted, suiting words to action with such admirable efficiency that Carly found herself seated at the dining-room table nursing a hot cup of delicious brew.

'Now, tell me what's wrong.'

Carly effected a faint shrugging gesture. 'I must be feeling my age,' she qualified with a faint smile. 'One late night through the week, and it takes me the next two to get over it.'

'OK,' Sarah accepted. 'So you don't want to talk. Now take these tablets.'

'Yes, Sister.'

'Don't be sassy with me, young woman. It won't work,' Sarah added with mock-severity.

'How was your date with James?' Carly queried in an attempt to divert the conversation away from herself.

'We had dinner, we talked, then he delivered me home.' Sarah lifted her shoulders in a non-committal gesture. 'It was all right, I guess.'

'That's it?' Carly looked slightly incredulous. '*All right* wraps it up?'

'OK, so he was the perfect gentleman.' Sarah's expression became pensive. 'I was surprised, that's all.'

James was beginning to sound more astute by the minute.

'He's asked me out to dinner next Saturday evening,' Sarah informed her quietly, and Carly applauded his perception in taking things slowly.

'He sounds nice.'

'I get the feeling he's streets ahead of me,' Sarah owned. 'Almost as if he knows what I'm thinking and how I'll react. It's—uncanny.'

Carly sipped her coffee and attempted to ignore her headache. It would take at least ten minutes before the pain began to ease, maybe another ten before it retreated to a dull heaviness that would only be alleviated by rest. After she dropped Ann-Marie at Susy's house, she'd come back and rest for an hour.

Sarah left a short while later, and Carly headed for a long leisurely shower, choosing to slip into tailored cotton trousers and a sleeveless top in eau-de-Nil silk. The pale colour looked cool and refreshing, and accentuated the deep auburn highlights of her hair and the clear honey of her skin.

Lunch was a light meal, for Ann-Marie was too excited to eat much in view of all the prospective fare available at Susy's party.

'Ready, darling?'

Ann-Marie's small features creased into an expression of excited anticipation, and Carly felt a tug on her heartstrings.

'Checklist time,' she bade lightly with a smile. 'Handkerchief? No last-minute need to visit the bathroom?'

'Yes,' Ann-Marie answered, retrieving a white linen square from the pocket of her dress. 'And I just did. Can we go now?'

'After you,' Carly grinned, sweeping her arm in the direction of the front door.

The drive was a relatively short one, for Susy lived in a neighbouring suburb, and in no time at all Carly brought the car to a halt behind a neat row of several parked cars.

'We're cutting the cake at three,' Susy's mother bade with an expressive smile. 'And I'm planning a reviving afternoon tea for the mothers at three-thirty while Susy opens her presents. I'd love you to be here if you can.'

Carly accepted the invitation, wished Susy 'Happy Birthday', then bent down to kiss Ann-Marie goodbye.

On returning home she garaged the car in its allotted space, sparing its slightly dusty paintwork a faint grimace as she closed and locked the door. Perhaps she could leave early and detour via a carwash.

The apartment seemed strangely empty, and she drifted into the kitchen to retrieve a cool drink from the refrigerator.

The buzz of the doorbell sounded loud in the silence of the apartment, and Carly frowned in momentary perplexity as she crossed the lounge. Sarah?

Instead, a tall, broad-shouldered, disturbingly familiar male frame filled the doorway.

The few seconds between recognition and comprehension seemed uncommonly long as she registered his dominating presence.

'What are you doing here?'

'Whatever happened to *hello*?' Stefano drawled, and his dry mocking tones sent an icy shiver down the length of her spine.

Her eyes sparked with visible anger, dark depths of sheer mahogany, and it irked her unbearably that she'd discarded her heeled sandals on entering the apartment, for it put her at a distinct disadvantage.

Impossibly tall, he towered head and shoulders above her, his impeccably tailored suit seeming incredibly formal on a day that was usually given to informality and relaxation.

Three nights ago his presence had shocked and dismayed her. Yesterday, she'd been momentarily numbed, grateful for the impartiality of his office. Now, there was no visible shield, no barrier, and she felt inordinately wary.

'Aren't you going to ask me in?'

He projected a dramatic mesh of elemental ruthlessness and primitive power, an intrinsic physical magnetism that teased her senses and rendered them intensely vulnerable.

Her chin lifted fractionally, her eyes locking with his, and she caught the lurking cynicism evident, almost as if he guessed the path her thoughts had taken and was silently amused by their passage.

'What if I refuse?' Brave words, given his sheer strength and indomitable will.

'Would you prefer an amicable discussion, or have me channel everything through my lawyers?'

His voice was deadly quiet, and she felt the cold clutch of fear.

'This isn't a convenient time.' She was mad, *insane* to thwart him continually, yet she was damned if she'd meekly stand aside and allow him entry into the privacy of her apartment.

His expression hardened, the assemblage of muscle and bone tautening into a chilling mask depicting controlled anger. 'You've just returned from delivering our daughter to a birthday party. How long before you need to collect her? An hour? Two?'

Sheer rage rushed to the surface, destroying any semblance of restraint. 'You've had me watched— *followed*?' Words momentarily failed her. 'You *bastard*,' she flung at last, sorely tempted to slam the door in his face, yet even as the thought occurred to her she negated the action as not only foolish but extremely dangerous.

For one infinitesimal second his eyes leapt with icy anger, then sharpened and became infinitely compelling as he raked her slender frame.

A shivery sensation feathered its way down the length of her spine as she fought against the intrinsic pull of his innate sexuality, and of its own volition her body seemed to flare into life as if ignited by some hidden combustible flame.

Seven years ago she'd gone willingly into his arms, his bed, and tasted every sensual delight in a sexual discovery that had set her on fire, enraptured by an ecstasy so acute that it hadn't seemed possible such pleasure existed. A passionate lover, he'd teasingly dispensed with each and every one of her inhibitions, and taught her to become so in tune with her own sensual being that each time they made love it was a total conflagration of the senses.

To deny him access to her apartment would gain absolutely nothing, and, drawing in a deep breath, she gathered her scattered emotions together as she aimed for contrived politeness.

'Please,' Carly indicated as she gestured towards two sofas and a chair in the small lounge. 'Sit down.'

Stefano chose to ignore the directive, and moved slowly across the room to examine a large frame containing a montage of small snapshots showing Ann-Marie in various stages of development from birth to as recently as a month ago.

A palpable silence filled the room until it enveloped everything. A silence so incredibly damning that it was almost tangible.

At long last he turned towards her, his eyes so remarkably dark that it was impossible to discern anything from his expression. 'Why did you choose not to tell me you were pregnant?' he began with deceptive softness.

Her throat felt impossibly dry, and so constricted that she doubted if her larynx could cope with emitting so much as a sound. 'If I had, you would have hauled me back to Perth,' she said at last.

'Indeed,' Stefano agreed. 'And I wouldn't now brand you a thief for stealing from me the first six years of my daughter's life.'

'If you'd had sufficient respect for our marriage, I wouldn't have felt compelled to leave,' she managed carefully. There was an inherent integrity apparent, a strength that came from deep within.

'And rehashing the past has no relevance to Ann-Marie's future.'

She could feel his anger emanating through the pores of his skin, and all her fine body hairs rose in protective self-defence. He could have shaken her to within an inch of her life, and taken extreme pleasure in her pain. It was there in his eyes, the tautly bunched muscles as he held himself rigidly in control. The promise of retribution was thinly veiled, and she felt immeasurably afraid, aware that such punishment would be swift and without warning—an utter devastation. But not yet, she reasoned shakily. A superb tactician, he would derive infinite satisfaction from playing out her fear.

'You've reached a decision?'

Her heart stopped, then clamoured into a thudding beat. 'Yes.' One look at his hard, obdurate features was sufficient to ascertain his inflexibility.

'Must I draw it from you like blood from stone?' he pursued, his voice assuming a deadly softness, and her eyes flared with resentment.

'I won't allow Ann-Marie to be a metaphorical bone we fight over in a lawcourt,' she said hardily. 'Nor will I put her through the emotional trauma of being bandied back and forth between two parents.' Her head lifted slightly and her chin tilted with determination. 'However, I have one condition.'

One eyebrow slanted in silent cynicism. 'And what is that?'

'You give up your women friends.'

He looked at her for what seemed an age, and she was conscious of an elevated nervous tension as the silence between them stretched to an unbearable length.

'Could you be more specific?'

'Lovers,' she said tightly, hating him.

'Does that mean you are prepared to accommodate me in bed?' he pursued with deadly softness.

Her heart stopped, then clamoured into a thudding beat at the memory his words evoked, and the nights when she'd behaved like a mindless wanton in his passionate embrace. With concentrated effort she managed to keep her gaze steady. 'No, it doesn't, damn you!'

Stefano remained silent, his eyes watchful as he witnessed the fleeting change of her emotions, then after a measurable silence he ventured silkily, 'You expect me to remain celibate?'

Of its own volition, her hand lifted to her hair and eased a stray tendril behind on ear, the gesture unconscious and betraying her inner nervousness. 'I'll live in the same house,' she declared quietly. 'I'll play at being your social hostess. For Ann-Marie's sake, I'll pretend everything between us is fine.' Her eyes were wide, clear, and filled with resolution. 'But I refuse to share your bed.'

The edge of his mouth lifted in a gesture of musing mockery. 'I shall insist you share the same room.'

'Why?' Carly demanded baldly.

His eyes speared hers, their depths hard and inflexible. 'Because I choose never to lose.'

'Our marriage meant nothing to you!'

'You think not?' Stefano countered with unmatched cynicism. 'I retain a clear memory of your...' He paused imperceptibly, then added mockingly, 'Contentment.'

'You gave me beautiful things, put me in a beautiful home, took me out to beautiful parties where beautiful people mingled and made out they were friends.' She felt incredibly sad. 'Except nothing was beautiful. Not really. I was a new playmate, someone you could show off when the occasion demanded.' Her eyes clouded, and her lashes fluttered down to form a protective veil. 'I was too young, too naïve, and I didn't know the rules.'

His expression hardened, and only a fool would choose to disregard the element of tensile steel beneath his sophisticated veneer, for apparent was a sense of purpose, a formidability that was infinitely daunting.

'And now you do?' he taunted silkily.

Her eyes were remarkably clear and steady, her resolve derived from an inner strength she would never allow him to destroy. 'I care for my daughter more than life itself,' she vowed quietly. 'Her health and well-being take precedence over anything you can throw at me.'

His eyes reflected an indomitable strength of will, and, unless she was mistaken, a chilling degree of silent rage.

Self-preservation was a prime motivation, yet right at this instant she felt as vulnerable as a cornered vixen. 'I insist on continuing with my career— even if it's only on a part-time basis.'

He didn't display any emotion whatsoever, and she shivered, aware of the force she was dealing with.

'You'll take an extended leave of absence, effective almost immediately, until Ann-Marie has recovered fully from surgery and is able to return to school.'

An angry flush crept over her cheeks as she fought to remain calm beneath his deliberate appraisal. 'It never entered my head to do otherwise,' she retaliated, determined to press home every point in her intention to set a personal precedent. 'However, I studied very hard to achieve my present position, and I have no intention of giving it up.'

'I'm sure Clive Mathorpe will be amenable to your working a reduced number of hours consistent with the time Ann-Marie spends at school.'

Cool, damning words, but carrying a weight she found impossible to ignore. She felt drained, emotionally and physically, and she needed to be alone.

'Will you please leave?'

'When do you collect Ann-Marie from the party?'

Carly's eyes flew to her watch, confirming with immeasurable relief that it was only minutes past three.

'Soon,' she acknowledged. 'I told Susy's mother I'd join her and the other mothers for afternoon tea.'

'In that case, I'll drive you there.'

A surge of anger rose to the surface, colouring her cheeks and sharpening her features. 'Damn you,' she cursed fiercely. 'I won't introduce you to Ann-Marie in one breath and reveal you're her father in the next!'

'Putting off the inevitable won't achieve anything,' Stefano stated in a voice that was infinitely dangerous. 'Invite me to dinner tonight.'

She closed her eyes, then slowly opened them again. 'Can't it wait a few days?'

'I've spoken to the specialist and arranged an appointment with the neurosurgeon for Tuesday. It's highly possible she'll undergo surgery within a week.' His gaze seemed incredibly dark as his features assumed a harsh, implacable mask. 'It's imperative that you're both established in my home as soon as possible. Emotional stability is crucial to her recuperation.'

'When she's fully recovered is soon enough,' Carly cried, hating the way he was taking charge.

'Tomorrow,' he informed her with diabolical insistence.

'No,' she denied at once. 'It will only cause her anxiety and add to the trauma of hospitalisation and surgery.'

'Use whatever guise you choose,' he insisted softly. 'But do it, Carly. Ann-Marie will soon accept I have a rightful place in her life—as she has in mine.'

A holiday, a brief stay, was the only tenable explanation, she decided, aware that Ann-Marie would probably view the proposal as something of an adventure.

'I'll be back at five,' he declared hardly. 'And I'll bring dinner. All you'll have to do is serve it.' His gaze seared her soul. 'Don't even think about running away, Carly,' he warned softly. 'This time, I'll search until I find you, and afterwards you'll wish you were dead.'

She stood transfixed as he turned and walked to the door, then quietly left the apartment.

It took ten minutes for her to regain some measure of composure, a further five before she took the lift down to the underground car park.

To sit with several other young mothers sipping tea and sharing party fare proved an anticlimax, and Carly felt as if she was operating on automatic pilot while her brain whirled off on a tangent.

She smiled a lot, and she even managed to laugh with apparent spontaneity at an amusingly told anecdote. Inside, she was a mess, conscious with every passing minute, each glance at Ann-Marie, of the impact Stefano would have on their lives. Especially her own.

The most pressing problem was finding the right words that would prevent Ann-Marie from forming any prejudice, one way or the other, about her mother's actions. Children were incredibly curious, and Ann-Marie was no exception.

For the following half-hour Carly watched Susy unwrap her presents, unable afterwards to remember more than a few, then, when the birthday cake was cut, she helped distribute the pieces.

Soon it was time to leave, and in the car she tussled with her conscience, agonising over how she should explain Stefano and their reconciliation, aware that the little girl was too excited after the party to really absorb much of what her mother had to say.

While driving a car in traffic was hardly the time or place, and as soon as they entered the apartment she plugged in the kettle, made herself a cup of strong tea, then settled down beside Ann-Marie on the sofa.

'Someone very special is going to have dinner with us tonight,' Carly began quietly, aware that she had her daughter's undivided attention by the bright curiosity evident in a pair of grey eyes that were identical to Stefano's.

'Sarah?'

'No, darling.' She hesitated slightly, then offered quietly, 'Your father.'

Ann-Marie's eyes widened measurably and her expression assumed a solemnity beyond her tender years. 'You said my father lived a long, long way away, and you left him before he knew about me.' The eyes grew even larger. 'Why didn't you want to tell him?'

Oh, dear lord. Out of the mouths of babes! 'Because we had an argument,' Carly answered honestly. 'And we said things we didn't mean.' An extension of the truth, for *she* had said them—Stefano hadn't uttered a single word in his defence.

'How did he find out about me?' Ann-Marie queried slowly.

'Your father moved to Sydney several months ago,' Carly said quietly, watching the expressive play of emotions evident. 'I've been in touch with him.'

'Why?'

If only there were a simple answer! 'I thought it was time he knew about you.'

Ann-Marie's gaze didn't waver, and it seemed an age before she spoke. 'And you don't not like him any more?'

She hid a sad smile at Ann-Marie's phraseology, and prayed the good lord would forgive her for the fabrication. 'No.'

'Now he wants to meet me,' Ann-Marie said with childish intuition, and Carly nodded her head in silent agreement, then endorsed,

'Yes, he does. Very much.'

'Is he angry with you for not telling him about me?'

'A little,' she admitted gently.

Ann-Marie's expression became comically fierce, and her chin jutted forward. 'If he's nasty to you, I'll hit him.'

The mental picture of a delicate, curly-haired six-year-old lashing out at a six-feet-plus male frame brought a slight smile to Carly's lips. 'That would be very rude, don't you think? Especially when he's a very kind man.' Not to her, never to her. However, she had no doubt he would be kind to his daughter.

'Does he want us to live together and be a family?'

Her answer had to be direct and without hesitation. 'Yes,' she said simply.

'Do *you* want us to live with him?' Ann-Marie persisted, and Carly felt as if she was caught in a trap with no way out.

'Yes.' Two untruths in the space of two minutes. If she wasn't careful, it could become a habit. 'Let's go and freshen up, shall we? He'll be here soon.'

'What do I call him?' Ann-Marie asked several minutes later as she stood quietly while Carly tidied her hair and redid her ribbons.

Carly had a terrible feeling the questions could only get worse! 'What would you like to call him?'

Ann-Marie appeared to deliberate, her eyes pensive as a slight frown creased her small brow. 'Daddy, I guess.' Her eyes moved to meet those of her mother in the mirror. 'Will I like him?'

She forced her mouth to widen into a warm smile, then she bent down to brush her lips against her daughter's temple. 'I'm sure that once you get to know him you'll like him very much,' she assured her quietly.

Ann-Marie looked at her mother's mirrored reflection and queried with puzzlement, 'Aren't you going to put some lipstick on?'

Carly didn't feel inclined to do anything to enhance her appearance, although she reached automatically for a slim plastic tube and outlined her mouth in clear red.

The sound of the doorbell heralded Stefano's arrival, and, catching hold of Ann-Marie's hand, she summoned a bright smile. 'Shall we answer that?'

I don't want to do this, a voice screamed silently from within, aware that the moment she opened the door her life would change irrevocably.

Carly schooled her features into an expression of welcome, and although she registered his physical presence she felt akin to a disembodied spectator.

Except that this was no nightmarish dream. Stefano Alessi represented reality, and she issued a greeting, aware that he had exchanged the formal business suit worn a few hours earlier for casual dark trousers and an open-necked shirt.

Carly barely hid a gasp of surprise as he reached out and threaded his fingers through hers, tightening them imperceptibly as she attempted to pull away from his grasp.

She registered a silent protest by digging the tips of her nails into hard bone and sinew. Not that it did any good, for he didn't even blink, and she watched in silence as his mouth curved into a warm smile.

Supremely conscious of Ann-Marie's intent gaze, she managed to return it, and she glimpsed the faint narrowing of his eyes, the silent warning evident an instant before they swept down to encompass his daughter.

'Hello, Ann-Marie.'

He made no attempt to touch her, and Ann-Marie looked at him solemnly for several long seconds, her eyes round and unwavering before they shifted to her mother, then back again to the man at her side.

'Hello,' she answered politely.

Carly felt as if her heart would tear in two, and she held her breath, supremely conscious of the man and the child, one so much a part of the other, both aware of their connection, yet each unsure quite how to proceed.

In a strange way, it allowed her to see a different side of the man, a hint of vulnerability evident that she doubted anyone else had ever witnessed. It surprised her, and made her wonder for one very brief minute how different things might have been if she'd stayed in the marriage, and if he would have given up Angelica Agnelli and assumed the role of devoted father.

A knife twisted deep within her, and the pain became intense at the thought of Stefano taking delight in all the changing facets of her pregnancy, the miracle of the birth itself, and the shared joy of their new-born child.

She'd denied him that, had felt justified in doing so, and if it hadn't been for Ann-Marie's illness she doubted that she'd ever have allowed him to become aware of his daughter's existence.

His fingers tightened around her own, almost as if he could read her thoughts, and she summoned the effort to move into the lounge, indicating one of two chairs.

'Please, take a seat.' Her voice sounded strange, not her own at all, and she extricated her hand from his, aware that it was only because he allowed her to do so.

'I hope you like chicken,' Stefano said, holding out a large carrier bag suitably emblazoned with an exclusive delicatessen logo. 'There's a variety of salads, some fresh bread rolls, cheese. And a bottle of wine.'

'Thank you,' Carly acknowledged with contrived warmth, and preceded him into the kitchen.

They ate at six, and Carly was aware of an inner tension that almost totally destroyed her appetite. There was no lull in conversation, and although Ann-Marie displayed initial reservation it wasn't long before she was chatting happily about school, her friends, Sarah, and how much she'd love to own a dog.

'I have a dog,' Stefano revealed, and Carly stifled a mental groan in the knowledge that he had just won a massive slice of Ann-Marie's interest, for the 'no animals allowed' rule enforced by the apartment managers ensured that tenants couldn't have pets.

Ann-Marie could barely hide her excitement. 'What sort of dog?'

Carly waited with bated breath, and had her worst fears confirmed with Stefano enlightened her. 'A Dobermann pinscher.'

'Mummy said that one day when we live in a house we can have a poodle.'

Stefano cast Carly a musing glance at her choice before turning his attention back to his daughter. 'In that case, we'll have to see about getting you one.'

It was bribery, pure and simple, and Carly hated him for it.

By the time Ann-Marie was settled happily in bed and asleep, it was clear that Stefano had succeeded in winning a place in his daughter's affections.

'I have to congratulate you,' Carly said quietly as she handed him some freshly made coffee. Then she crossed the small lounge and selected a chair as far distant from his as possible.

His gaze was startlingly level. 'On developing an empathy with my daughter?'

She met his eyes and held their gaze with all the force of her maternal instincts. 'If you do anything to hurt her—*ever*,' she emphasised softly, 'I'll kill you.'

He didn't speak for several long seconds, and Carly felt close to screaming point. 'You wanted for her to hate me?'

'*No*. No,' she repeated shakily, knowing that it wasn't true.

'Yet you decry the speed with which she has gifted me a measure of her affection,' Stefano pursued.

She refused to admit it, and stirred her coffee instead, wanting only for the evening to end so that she could be free of his disturbing presence.

'Gaining her trust won't be achieved overnight,' he discounted drily, adding, 'And love has to be earned.'

'Why agree to gift her a poodle?'

'I said *we* would have to see about getting her one,' he responded evenly, and she instantly flared,

'A Dobermann and a poodle both on the same property?'

'Prince is a well-trained guard dog who is exceptionally obedient. I doubt there will be a problem.'

'And it matters little to you that I might have a problem moving into your home?'

His eyes were hard, with no hint of any softness. 'I'm sure you'll manage to overcome it.'

Suddenly she'd had enough, and she replaced her cup down on the coffee-table, then rose to her feet. 'I'm tired and I'd like you to leave.'

He followed her movements with a lithe indolence, then covered the distance to the front door. 'Be packed and ready at midday. I'll collect you.'

She wanted to hit him, and she lifted her hand, only to have it caught in a merciless grip.

'Don't even think about it,' Stefano warned silkily. 'This time I won't be so generous.'

There could be little doubt about the veiled threat, and she looked at him in helpless anger, wanting so much to strike out in temper, yet forced to contain it out of consideration to a sleeping child who, should she wake and perchance witness such

a scene, would be both puzzled and frightened, and
unable to comprehend the cause.

Stefano released her hand, then he opened the
door and moved out into the foyer without so much
as a backward glance.

CHAPTER FOUR

CARLY experienced a sense of acute nervousness as she caught sight of Stefano's imposing double-storeyed French-château-style home. Situated in the exclusive suburb of Clontarf and constructed of grey stone, it sat well back from the road in beautifully kept grounds.

A spreading jacaranda tree in full bloom with its carpet of lilac flowers provided a fitting backdrop to an assortment of precision-clipped shrubs, and symmetrical borders filled with a variety of colourful flowers that were predominantly red, pink, white and yellow.

Dear lord, what had she *done*? The enormity of it all settled like a tremendous weight on her slim shoulders. In the space of fifteen hours she had packed, cleaned the apartment, notified the leasing agent, and confided in Sarah. *And* tossed and turned for the short time she'd permitted herself to sleep. Now she had to face reality.

The car drew to a halt adjacent to the main entrance, and no sooner had Stefano slid out from behind the wheel than a short, well-built man of middle years emerged from the house to retrieve several suitcases from the capacious boot.

'Joe Bardini,' Stefano told them as Carly and Ann-Marie slid from the car. 'Joe and his wife Sylvana look after the house and grounds.'

69

The man's smile was warm, and his voice when he spoke held the barest trace of an Italian accent. 'Sylvana is in the kitchen preparing lunch. I will tell her you have arrived.'

Some of Carly's tension transmitted itself to her daughter, for Ann-Marie's fingers tightened measurably within her own as Stefano led the way indoors.

The foyer was spacious, with cream-streaked marble tiles and delicate archways either side of a magnificent double staircase leading to the upper floor. The focal point was a beautiful crystal chandelier, spectacular in design by day. Carly could only wonder at its luminescence by night.

'Would you prefer to explore the house before or after lunch?'

'Can we now?' Ann-Marie begged before Carly had a chance to utter so much as a word, and Stefano cast his daughter a musing glance.

'Why not? Shall we begin upstairs?'

'Yes, please.'

They ascended one side of the curving staircase, and on reaching the upper floor he directed them left to two guest rooms and a delightful bedroom suite with a connecting bathroom.

'Is this where I'm going to sleep?' Ann-Marie asked as she looked at the softly toned bedcovers.

'Do you like it?' Stefano asked gently, and she nodded.

'It's very pretty. Can Sarah come visit sometimes?'

'Of course,' he answered solemnly.

'Sarah lives in the apartment next door,' Ann-Marie explained carefully. 'She is our very best friend.'

To the right of the central staircase Stefano opened a door leading into the main suite, and Carly's eyes flew to two queensize beds separated by a double pedestal. A spacious *en suite* was visible, and there was an adjoining sitting-room complete with soft leather chairs, a television console, and escritoire.

'We'll use this suite,' Stefano indicated, and Carly refrained from comment, choosing instead to shoot him a telling glance as she preceded him to the head of the stairs.

If he thought she'd share the same bedroom with him, he had another think coming!

Once downstairs he led them into a formal lounge containing items of delicate antique furniture, deep-seated sofas and single chairs, employing a visually pleasing mix of cream, beige and soft sage-green. Oil-paintings graced the walls, a sparkling crystal chandelier hung suspended from a beautiful fili-gree-plastered ceiling, and wide floor-to-ceiling sliding glass doors opened out on to a covered terrace.

Even at a glance it was possible to see the blue-tiled swimming-pool beyond the terrace, and catch a glimpse of the magnificent view out over the harbour.

The formal dining-room was equally impressive, and his study held an awesome arsenal of high-tech equipment as well as a large mahogany desk, and wall-to-wall bookshelves.

The southern wing comprised an informal family room, dining-room and an enormous kitchen any chef would kill for.

A pleasantly plump middle-aged woman turned as they entered, and her kindly face creased into a warm welcoming smile as Stefano effected introductions.

'Lunch will be ready in ten minutes,' Sylvana declared.

'Is Prince outside? Can I see him?' Ann-Marie asked, and she made no objection when Stefano reached forward and caught hold of her hand.

'Come and be properly introduced.'

The dog was huge, and looked incredibly fearsome, yet beneath Stefano's guidance he became a docile lamb, his eyes large and soulful, his whimpering enthusiasm as close to canine communication as it was possible to get.

'After lunch we'll take him for a walk round the grounds, and you can watch him go through his paces.'

Lunch was served in the informal dining-room, and Ann-Marie did justice to the tender roast chicken with accompanying vegetables, as well as the delicious crème caramel dessert.

The excellent glass of white wine Carly sipped through lunch helped soothe her fractured nerves, and afterwards she walked quietly with Ann-Marie as Stefano led the Dobermann through a series of commands.

It was very warm outdoors, and Carly glimpsed a few tell-tale signs of her daughter's tiredness. The symptoms of her condition could descend with little warning, and it was essential that her reserves of strength were not overtaxed.

'Shall we go upstairs?' Carly suggested, catching hold of Ann-Marie's hand. 'You can lie down while I unpack your clothes.'

Stefano shot her a quick glance, his expression pensive as Ann-Marie stumbled slightly.

'Can I see Prince again before dinner?'

'Of course. You can watch Joe feed him.'

Carly lifted her into her arms, and Ann-Marie nestled her head into the curve of her mother's shoulder, her small hands lifting to link together around Carly's neck.

'Let me take her,' Stefano bade quietly, and Carly made to demure, barely able to control her surprise as Ann-Marie allowed Stefano to transfer her into his arms without protest.

Ann-Marie fought against encroaching lassitude as they made their way indoors, and by the time Stefano deposited her gently down on to the bed she was asleep.

His eyes were dark and slightly hooded as he watched Carly deftly remove the little girl's shoes then draw up a light cover before crossing to the window to close the curtains.

'She just needs to rest,' she said quietly. 'She'll be all right in an hour or two.'

Carly turned and walked from the room, supremely conscious of a distinct prickling sensation feathering her spine as he followed close behind.

It was damnable to be so aware of him, and in the hallway she quickened her step towards the main suite. 'I'll begin unpacking.' Her voice sounded incredibly stilted and polite, almost dismissing, for he had the power to ruffle her composure more than she was prepared to admit.

Their combined luggage was stacked neatly on the floor, and her eyes swept the room, hating the invidious position in which she'd been placed and the man who deliberately sought to put her there.

'Afraid, Carly?' a deep voice drawled from behind, and she turned slowly to face him, her eyes steady.

'You intend me to be,' she said with hesitation, aware of an inner resentment. 'This is part of a diabolical game, isn't it?' she flared, on a verbal rollercoaster. 'Separate beds, but having to share the same room. An *en suite* with no lock, ensuring you can invade my privacy any time you choose.' A degree of bitterness made itself apparent. 'And you will choose, won't you, Stefano? Just for the hell of it.' Her eyes darkened measurably, the gold flecks appearing like chips of topaz against brown velvet. 'Don't ever mistake your bed for mine,' she warned with deadly softness. 'I'd mark you for life.'

His gaze raked hers, harsh and unrelenting. 'Be grateful I've allowed you a separate bed,' he drawled smoothly. 'It wasn't my original intention.'

Her heart lurched, then missed a beat as sensation unfurled deep within her, the pain so acute that she almost gasped at its intensity. For one horrifying moment she held a clear vision of their bodies locked in lovemaking, aware that if he chose to take her now it would be a violation motivated by revenge.

Her eyes grew large, expressing a mixture of shock and anger, yet she refused to be subjugated to him in any way. 'Rape, even between husband

and wife,' she reminded stiltedly, 'is a criminal offence.'

Something flickered in the depths of his eyes, then it was successfully masked. 'You know me well enough to understand that rape would never be a consideration.'

No, she thought shakily. He was too skilled a lover to harm his partner with any form of physical pain. His revenge would be infinitely more subtle.

As it had been on one previous occasion, when she'd driven him to anger with a heated accusation she'd refused to retract or explain, and he had simply hauled her unceremoniously over his shoulder and carried her into the bedroom where he had conducted a deliberate leisurely assault on her senses until she was on fire with a desire so intense that she had possessed no reason, no sanity, only base animal need and a wild driven hunger for the release that only he could give. Except that he had taken pleasure in making her wait until she was reduced to begging unashamedly like a craven wanton caught in the throes of some primeval force, and then, only then, had he taken her with a merciless mastery that knew no bounds in a totally erotic plundering of her senses. With no energy left to move, she'd drifted into sleep, only to waken in the early morning hours, where self-loathing had surfaced, and a degree of shame. It had been the catalyst that had motivated her to leave.

Carly shivered suddenly, hating him more than she thought it was possible to hate anyone, and she watched in silence as he crossed to a concealed wall-safe, activated the mechanism, then removed a

small jeweller's box before covering the distance
between with calm, leisurely steps.

'Your rings,' Stefano declared, extracting the exquisite square-cut diamond with its baguette-cut
diamond mounting, and its matching band.

Surprise momentarily widened her eyes as she recalled tearing both from her finger in a fit of angry
rage. 'You kept them?'

His gaze was remarkably steady. 'What did you
expect me to do with them?'

She was lost for words, her mobile features
hauntingly expressive for a few seconds before she
schooled them into restrained reserve, unable in the
few ensuing seconds to make any protest as he took
hold of her left hand and slid both rings in place.

Of their own volition her fingers sought the large
stone, twisting it back and forth in a gesture that
betrayed an inner nervousness.

His proximity disturbed her more than she was
prepared to admit, and she was aware of a watchful
quality in his stance, an intentness so overpowering
that she felt almost afraid.

Her whole body stirred, caught up in a web of
sensuality so acute that it seemed as if every vein,
every nerve cell in her body flamed in electrifying
recognition of *his*, which was totally opposite to
the dictates of her brain.

To continue standing here like this was madness,
and without a further word she turned away from
him, crossing to her luggage to begin the chore of
unpacking.

Carly's movements were steady and unhurried as
she placed clothes on hangers in a capacious walk-

in wardrobe, and she was aware of the instant he turned and left the room.

Dinner was a simple meal comprising minestrone followed by pasta, and afterwards Sylvana served coffee in the informal lounge.

Settling Ann-Marie to bed was achieved without fuss, and Stefano willingly agreed to his daughter's request to listen to a bedtime story.

A novelty, Carly assured herself as she chose the opposite side of Ann-Marie's bed, conscious that she was the focus of two pair of eyes—one pair loving and direct, the other musing and faintly speculative.

Forget he's there, a tiny voice prompted as she picked up the book and began to read. Who do you think you're kidding? another derided.

Somehow Carly managed to inject her voice with its customary warmth and enthusiasm, and she had almost finished when Ann-Marie's eyes fluttered down.

Minutes later Stefano rose quietly to his feet and waited at the door for Carly to precede him from the room.

'Does she usually wake in the night?' he queried as they neared the head of the stairs, and Carly shook her head.

'Very rarely.' She was a nervous wreck, she had a headache, and all she wanted to do was have a long leisurely shower, then slip into bed. She said as much, adding, 'I'll drop Ann-Marie at school in the morning, then go into the office for a few hours.'

'Clive Mathorpe isn't expecting you,' Stefano drawled, and she felt a *frisson* of alarm at his long hard glance. 'I've already enlightened him that his highly regarded Carly Taylor is Carly Taylor *Alessi*.'

Anger surged to the surface at his high-handedness. 'How dare you?' she vented in softly voiced fury. 'I am quite capable of telling him myself!'

'As my wife, there's no necessity for you to work. Your first priority lies with Ann-Marie.' The velvet smoothness in his voice should have been sufficient warning, but she was too stubborn to take any heed.

'I agree,' she conceded, determined to win points against him. 'However, as she'll be at school from eight forty-five until two-thirty, I don't see why I shouldn't spend those hours delegating work to whoever will take my place over the next few weeks.'

'I'll allow you tomorrow,' Stefano agreed hardly. 'But that's all.'

'Don't begin dictating what I can and can't do!' Carly said fiercely. She felt defensive, and very, very angry. 'And don't you *dare* imply that I'm an irresponsible mother! What sort of father will *you* be?' she demanded. 'It isn't nearly enough to provide a child with a beautiful home and numerous possessions. The novelty soon wears off when you can't be present at the school fête, or attend the end-of-year play.' Her eyes flashed with fiery topaz as her anger deepened. 'What happens next week, the week after that, and all the long months ahead?' she queried fiercely. 'You'll be too busy jetting off to God knows where, cementing yet another multi-million-dollar deal. When you *are* home, you'll probably leave in the morning before she wakes, and return long after she's given up any hope of catching a glimpse of you. How am I going to explain that your liaison with fatherhood will be conducted by remote control?'

His eyes were dark and unfathomable, and she was aware of a degree of anger apparent. 'Why are you so sure it will be?'

'Because you lead such a high-profile existence,' she flung in cautiously. 'It can't be any other way, damn you!'

He looked at her in silence for what seemed an age, and it was all she could do to hold his gaze. Yet she wouldn't subvert her own beliefs in deference to a man whose credo was different from her own.

'Tell me, are you staging a fight as a matter of principle, or merely as an attempt to vent some of your rage?'

'Both!'

'With any clear thought to the consequences?' Stefano pursued, his eyes never leaving hers for a second.

'Don't you dare threaten me!'

One dark eyebrow rose in cynical query. 'If you imagine I'll take any invective you choose to throw in my direction without retaliation, you're mistaken,' he warned silkily.

Carly felt as if she was on a rollercoaster leading all the way down to hell. 'I'm damned if I'll play happy families at a flick of your fingers!'

'I doubt you'll do or say anything to upset Ann-Marie.'

He was right. She wouldn't. Yet she desperately wanted to hit out at him for invading her life and turning it upside-down.

'Do you enjoy the power it gives you to use my daughter as an excuse to blackmail me?'

'Are you making an allegation?' Stefano countered in a voice that would have quelled an adversary.

For a few fateful seconds they seemed locked in silent battle, and she felt as if she was shattering into a thousand pieces. 'It's the truth!'

He stood regarding her in silence, his eyes darkly inscrutable, yet there was an air of leashed anger apparent, a sense of control that was almost frightening.

'Quit while you're ahead, Carly.'

She felt the need to be free of him, and preferably alone. For a few hours at least. 'I'm going to take a shower and watch television for a while.'

One eyebrow rose fractionally. 'A desire for solitude?'

'I'm off duty,' she declared, uncaring of his reaction.

'Careful with your claws, my little cat,' Stefano warned softly. 'Or I may choose to unsheathe my own.'

There was nothing she could add, so she didn't even try. Instead, she turned and walked towards their suite, and once inside she carefully closed the door.

He didn't follow, and she moved into the *en suite* and shed her clothes, then took a long shower, and, towelled dry, she pulled on a thin cotton shift and emerged into the bedroom, to stand hesitantly, unsure which of the two beds she should occupy.

Dammit, she swore softly. With her luck, she'd choose the wrong one, and then Stefano would be cynically amused by her mistake.

There was only one solution, and she caught up a towelling robe and slid it on, then walked through to the sitting-room, activated the television, and sank into a comfortable chair.

If necessary, she determined vengefully, she'd sleep here, rather than slip into the wrong bed!

Sunday evening television offered the choice of three movies, an intellectual book review, or a play spoken entirely in Hungarian. A karate-kickboxer epic wasn't her preferred viewing, nor was a terminator blockbuster, and she wasn't in the mood for a chilling thriller. After switching channels several times, she simply selected one for the sake of it and allowed her attention to wander.

At some stage she must have dozed, for she was aware of a strange sense of weightlessness, a desire to sink more comfortably into arms that seemed terribly familiar.

A small sigh escaped her lips, and she burrowed her face into the curve of a hard, muscular shoulder, then lifted her hands to encircle a male neck.

It felt so good, so *right*, and she murmured her appreciation. Her lips touched against warm skin, moving involuntarily as they savoured a texture and scent her subconscious recognised—not only recognised, but delighted in the discovery.

Except that she wanted more, and the tip of her tongue ventured out in a tentative exploratory tasting, edging up a deeply pulsing cord in search of a mouth she instinctively knew could bestow pleasure.

Then the barriers between unconsciousness and awareness began to disperse, bringing a horrifying knowledge that, although the arms that held her belonged to the right man, it was the wrong time, the wrong room, and her dream-like state owed nothing to the reality!

For a moment her eyes retained a warm luminescence, a musing witchery, then they clouded with pain before being hidden by two thickly lashed veils as she struggled to be free of him.

'Put me down!'

'I was about to,' Stefano drawled as he placed her between fragrantly clean sheets, and her lashes swept up to reveal intense anger.

His touch was impersonal, yet she felt as if she was on fire, with every separate nerve-end quivering into vibrant life, each individual skin-cell an ambivalent entity craving his touch.

Carly snatched the top sheet and pulled it up to her chin in a defensive gesture. 'Get away from me!'

His eyes speared hers, darkly mesmeric as she forced herself not to look away.

'You're as nervous as a kitten,' he drawled musingly. 'Why, when we've known each other in the most intimate sense?'

Reaching out, he brushed gentle fingers down the length of her cheek to the edge of her mouth, then traced the curving contour with a stray forefinger. 'What are you afraid of, *cara*?'

'Nothing,' Carly responded carefully. 'Absolutely nothing at all.'

Liar, she derided silently. No matter how hard she tried she was unable to still the fast-beating

pulse that hummed through her veins, seducing
every nerve and fibre until she felt incredibly *alive*.

His smile was wholly cynical, and his eyes held
a gleam of mockery as they conducted a deliberately slow appraisal of her expressive features,
lingering over-long on the visible pulsebeat at the
base of her throat before travelling up to meet her
gaze.

'Goodnight, Carly,' he bade her lazily. 'Sleep
well.'

She mutinously refused to comment, and she
watched as he turned and walked from the room.
Damn him, she cursed silently. She *wouldn't* sleep
in this bed, this room!

Anger fuelled her resolve, and she flung aside
the covers, grabbed hold of her robe, then retreated quietly to an empty suite near by.

It held a double bed—made up in readiness, she
discovered—and she slid beneath the covers, then
switched off the bedside lamp.

Quite what Stefano's reaction would be when he
found her missing wasn't something she gave much
thought to for a while. She was too consumed with
numerous vengeful machinations, all designed to
cause him harm.

By the time she focused on what he might do,
she was drifting off to sleep, too comfortable and
too tired to care.

At some stage during the night she came sharply
awake as a light snapped on, and she blinked
against its brightness, disorientated by her surroundings for one brief second before realisation
dawned. Except that by then it was too late to do

anything but struggle as hard hands lifted her un-ceremoniously to her feet.

The face above her own was set in frightening lines, jaw clenched, mouth compressed into a savagely thin line, and eyes as dark as obsidian slate burning with controlled anger.

'You can walk,' Stefano drawled with dangerous softness. 'Or I can carry you.' His eyes hardened with chilling intensity, and Carly felt immensely afraid. 'The choice is yours.'

He resembled a dark brooding force—lethal, she acknowledged shakily, noting a leashed quality in his stance that boded ill should she dare consider rebellion.

'I won't share the same bedroom with you,' she ventured with a brave attempt at defiance, and saw his eyes narrow for an instant before they began a deliberately slow raking appraisal of her slim curves.

It was terrifying, for her skin flamed as if he'd actually trailed his fingers along the same path, and her eyes filled with futile rage. Her fingers curled into her palms, the knuckles showing white as she restrained herself from lashing out at him.

'We agreed to a reconciliation,' he reminded her with icy detachment. 'For Ann-Marie's benefit.' His dark gaze seared hers, then struck at her heart. 'I think we each realise our daughter is sufficiently intelligent to know that happily reconciled parents don't maintain separate bedrooms.' He knew just how to twist the knife, and he did it without hesitation. 'Are you prepared for the questions she'll pose?'

Carly's slim form shook with anger, and her eyes blazed with it as she held his gaze. 'If you so much as touch me,' she warned as she collected her wrap and slipped it on, 'I'll fight you all the way down to hell.'

It took only seconds to reach the master suite, and only a few more to discard her wrap and slip into one of the two beds dominating the large room. With determination she turned on to her side and closed her eyes, uncaring whether he followed her or not.

She heard him enter the room and the soft decisive snap as the door closed, followed by the faint rustle of clothes being discarded, then the room was plunged into darkness, and she lay still, her body tense, until sheer exhaustion triumphed and she fell asleep.

Monday rapidly shaped up to be one of those days where Murphy's Law prevailed, Carly decided grimly, for whatever could go wrong did, from a ladder in her tights to a traffic jam *en route* to the city.

On reaching the office, there appeared to be little improvement. She didn't even manage coffee mid-morning, and lunch was a salad sandwich she sent out for and washed down quickly with apple juice as she checked and double-checked details required urgently for an eminent client.

Given normal circumstances she excelled under pressure, regarding it as a challenge rather than nerve-destroying, and it was with mixed feelings that she tidied her desk, took leave of her col-

leagues and drove to collect Ann-Marie from
school.

They arrived at Stefano's elegant mansion—
Carly refused to call it home—shortly after three
to find a silver-grey BMW standing in the driveway

'For you,' Joe Bardini informed Carly as he
emerged from the house to greet them. 'Mr Alessi
had it delivered this morning.'

Had he, indeed! 'It's very nice, Joe,' she ac-
corded quietly, and she veiled her eyes so that he
wouldn't see the anger evident.

'Mr Alessi suggested you might like to take it for
a test drive.'

She managed a warm smile, and indicated her
briefcase. 'I think I'll get changed first.'

'It's really hot,' Ann-Marie declared as she followed Carly indoors. 'Can we go for a swim?'

Ten minutes later they were laughing and
splashing together in the shallow end of the pool
and after half an hour Carly persuaded her daughter
to emerge on the pretext of having a cool drink.

'Look,' Ann-Marie alerted her from the pool's
edge. 'Daddy's home.' The name slid so easily, so
naturally off the little girl's tongue, with no hesitation or reservation whatsoever, and Carly felt her
stomach clench with pain.

She was suddenly supremely conscious of the
simply styled maillot, and, although it was perfectly respectable when dry, wet, it clung lovingly
to soft curves. Much too lovingly, she saw with
dismay, conscious of the way it hugged her breasts.

Slowly she turned to face him, a faint false smile
pulling at the edges of her mouth as she wound a
towel around Ann-Marie's small frame, then she

quickly reached for another, draping it over one shoulder in the hope that it would provide some sort of temporary cover.

Her action amused him, and she met his gaze with equanimity, heighteningly aware of his studied appraisal and her own damning reaction.

It was difficult to keep the smile in place, but she managed—just. If she'd been alone she would have slapped his face.

It was perhaps as well that he turned his attention to his daughter, whose wide, solemn eyes switched from one parent to the other as she assessed his show of affection and her mother's reaction.

Consequently Carly presented a relaxed façade, deliberately injecting some warmth as she enquired as to his day, and commented on his early return.

'I thought we might drive out to one of the beaches for a barbecue,' Stefano suggested, and was immediately rewarded with Ann-Marie's enthusiastic response.

'Can we go in the new car?'

His answering smile was her reward. 'I don't see why not.'

There was no way Carly could demur, and with a few words and a fixed smile she directed her daughter upstairs to shower and change.

It was after five when Stefano drove the BMW out of the driveway and headed towards one of the northern beaches, where he played chef, cooking steak and sausages to perfection while Carly busied herself setting out a variety of salads, sliced a freshly baked French breadstick, and enjoyed a light wine spritzer.

The air was fresh and clean, slightly tangy with the smell of the sea. A faint warm breeze drifted in from the ocean, teasing the length of her hair, and she gazed out to the horizon, seeing deep blue merge with clear azure, aware in that moment of a profound feeling of awe for the magnitude and greatness of nature. There was a sense of time-lessness, almost an awareness that life was ex-tremely tenuous, gifted by some powerful deity, and that each day, each hour, should be seized for the enjoyment of its beauty.

Tears welled at the backs of her eyes and threatened to spill. Dear God, what would she do if anything happened to Ann-Marie? How could she cope?

'Mummy, what's wrong?'

Carly caught her scattered thoughts together and summoned a smile. 'I'm admiring the view,' she explained, and, reaching down, she lifted Ann-Marie into her arms and directed her attention out over the ocean. 'Look, isn't that a ship in the distance?'

They ate sausages tasting faintly of smoke, tender steak, and the two adults washed it all down with a light fruity wine, then they packed everything back into the boot of the car and walked along the foreshore.

Ann-Marie chattered happily, pausing every now and then to inspect and collect seashells, which she presented for Carly's inspection, then when she grew tired Stefano lifted her high to sit astride his shoulders, and they made their way slowly back to the car.

A gentle breeze tugged at Carly's long cotton skirt and teased the length of her hair. The sun's warmth was beginning to cool as the giant orb sank lower in the sky, its colour flaring brilliantly as it changed from yellow to gold to orange, then to a deep rose before sinking below the horizon. The keening sea-gulls quietened, and took their last sweeping flight before seeking shelter for the night.

There was a sense of peace and tranquillity, almost a feeling of harmony with the man walking at her side, and for a moment she wondered if their marriage could have worked... Then she dismissed it in the knowledge that there were too many 'if only's. There was only *now*.

'You take the wheel,' Stefano instructed as they reached the car, and Carly shook her head, unwilling to familiarise herself with a new vehicle while he sat in the passenger seat. 'I insist,' he added quietly, and in Ann-Marie's presence she had little option but to accede.

It was almost nine when they arrived home, and Ann-Marie was so tired that she fell asleep almost as soon as her head touched the pillow.

CHAPTER FIVE

'COFFEE?' Stefano queried as they descended the staircase, and Carly nodded her head in silent acquiescence.

In the kitchen she filled the percolator with water, selected a fresh filter, spooned in a measure of freshly ground coffee-beans, then activated the machine before reaching for two cups and saucers, sugar.

'From now on, use the BMW.'

Resentment flared in his mocking command. 'There's nothing wrong with my car,' she retaliated at once. 'It's roadworthy and reliable.'

His gaze trapped hers and she felt every single hair on her body prickle with inexplicable foreboding. 'When was it last fully serviced?'

Too long ago, Carly admitted silently, all too aware that over the past few months all her money had gone on expensive medical bills.

'You don't like the BMW?' Stefano queried with deceptive mildness, and she summoned a false smile.

'I presume it's the "in" vehicle that wives of wealthy corporate directors are driving this year.'

His eyes narrowed fractionally, and the edges of his mouth curved with cynicism. 'That wasn't the reason I chose it.'

'No?' Her faint smile was tinged with mockery. 'It does, however, fit the required image.'

'And what is that, Carly?' Stefano pursued with dangerous softness.

'You're a very successful man,' she returned solemnly, 'who has to be seen to surround himself with the trappings of success.' She lifted an expressive hand and effected an encompassing gesture. 'This house, the cars. Even the women who grace a part of your life.'

His eyes locked with hers, and she suppressed a faint shivery sensation at the dark implacability evident.

'You know nothing of the women in my life.'

It was like a knife twisting deep inside her heart, and she fought visibly to contain the pain. She even managed to dredge up a smile as his eyes seared hers, dark, brooding, and infinitely hard.

Carly felt as if she couldn't breathe, and the beat of her heart seemed to thud right through her chest, fast-paced and deafening in its intensity. She wanted to escape—from the room, the man, the *house*. Except that she had to stay. For a while, at least. Until Ann-Marie was fully recovered. Then . . .

'The coffee is ready.'

His voice intruded, and she turned blindly towards the coffee-machine. Dear God, she doubted her ability to walk the few paces necessary and calmly pour the brew into cups, let alone drink from one. She'd probably scald her mouth, or drop the cup. Maybe both.

'I no longer feel like any,' she managed in a voice that sounded indistinct and far removed from her own.

'Add a dash of brandy, and cream,' Stefano ordered steadily. 'It will help you sleep.'

She opened her mouth to respond, only to have him pursue with dangerous softness, 'Don't argue.'

'I'm not arguing!'

'Then stop wasting energy on being so stubbornly determined to oppose me.'

'You must know how much I hate being here,' she flung with restrained anger. She was so infuriated that it took every ounce of control not to lash out at him.

'Almost as much as you hate me,' Stefano drawled imperturbably as he moved to pour the coffee, then he added brandy and cream to both cups.

'You have no intention of making things easy for me, do you?' Carly demanded bitterly.

His eyes assumed a chilling bleakness, his features assembling into a hard, inflexible mask. 'You're treading a mental tightrope.' He lifted a hand and caught hold of her chin, his fingers firm and faintly cruel. 'And I'm in no mood to play verbal games.'

'Then stop treating me like a fractious child.' It was a cry from within, heartfelt, and more revealing than she intended.

'Start behaving like a woman and I'll respond accordingly,' he said hardly, and flecks of fiery topaz lightened the darkness of her eyes.

'Close my mind and open my legs?' Rage bubbled to the surface and erupted without thought to the consequence. 'Sorry, Stefano. I'm not that desperate.'

For a moment she thought he meant to strike her, and she was powerless to escape him as hard hands curled round her arms and pulled her close.

'This time,' he ground out grimly, 'you push me too far.'

He possessed sufficient strength to do her grievous bodily harm, yet she stood defiant, unwilling to retract or apologise for so much as a single word.

With slow deliberation he caught both her hands together, then slid one hand beneath her head, tilting it as he impelled her forward, then his mouth was on hers, hard and possessively demanding.

A silent scream rose and died in her throat, and she began to struggle, hating him with all her heart as he exerted sufficient pressure to force open her mouth, then his tongue became a pillaging destructive force that had her silently begging him to stop.

His stance altered, and one hand splayed down over the gentle swell of her bottom, pressing her close in against him so that the heat of his arousal was a potent virile force that was impossible to ignore.

The invasion of her mouth didn't lessen, and she felt absorbed, overwhelmed, *possessed* by a man who would refuse anything other than her complete capitulation.

Something snapped inside her, swamping her with anger and a need for retribution. She began to struggle more fiercely, managing to free one hand, which she balled into a fist to flail against his back. She clenched her jaw against the considerable force of his, and gained a minor victory when she managed to capture his tongue with her teeth.

Not enough to inflict any damage, but sufficient to cause him to still fractionally, then he was free, but only momentarily, for he lifted her effortlessly over one shoulder and strode from the room.

'You bastard,' Carly hissed vehemently as she pummelled her fists against the hard muscles of his back. 'Put me down, damn you!'

She fought so hard that she lost all sense of direction, and it wasn't until he began to ascend the central staircase that she began to feel afraid. Her struggles intensified, without success, and several seconds later she heard the solid clunking sound of the bedroom door as it closed behind them, then without ceremony she was lowered down to her feet.

Defiance blazed from her expressive features as she met his hardened gaze, and despite their compelling intensity she refused to bow down to fear. Her mouth felt violated, her tongue sore, the delicate tissues grazed and swollen. Even her throat ached, and her jaw.

'If it weren't for Ann-Marie...' She trailed to a halt, too incensed to continue.

'Precisely,' Stefano agreed succinctly. His implication was intentional, and she burst into voluble speech.

'You're so damned *ruthless*,' Carly accused vengefully. 'You dominate everything, *everyone*. I can't wait to be free of you.'

He went completely still, and she was vividly reminded of a superb jungle animal she'd viewed on a television documentary; of the encapsulated moment when every muscle in his body had tensed prior to the fatal spring that captured and annihilated his prey. Stefano looked just as dangerous, portraying the same degree of leashed violence.

'You believe our reconciliation to be temporary?' he queried in a voice that sounded like the finest silk being torn asunder.

She drew in a deep breath, then slowly released it. 'When Ann-Marie is completely recovered, I intend to file for divorce.'

His eyes lanced hers, killing in their intensity. 'You honestly believe I'd allow you to attempt to take her away from me?'

'Dear lord in heaven,' Carly breathed shakily. 'Who do you think you are? *God*?'

He was silent for so long that she thought he didn't mean to answer, then he drawled with deliberate softness, 'I have the power to hound you through every lawcourt in the country for whatever reason I choose to nominate.'

She felt sickened, and *raw* with immeasurable pain. 'Are you so bent on revenge that you'd punish yourself as well as me?'

His eyes raked her slim frame. 'Punish? Aren't you being overly fanciful?'

'Angelica Agnelli. I imagine she still——' She paused fractionally, then continued with deliberate emphasis, '*Liaises* with you?'

His voice was tensile steel, and just as dangerous. 'In a professional capacity—yes.'

'And is she still based in Perth?' Carly pursued unrepentantly. 'Or has she also moved to Sydney?'

'Sydney.'

'I see,' she said dully, and wondered at her own stupidity in querying if the relationship between Stefano and Angelica still existed. It hadn't ceased and probably never would.

'Do you?' Stefano queried, and she smiled with infinite sadness, all the fight in her suddenly gone.

'Oh, yes,' she assented wearily. 'I was way out of my league right from the beginning.'

'You should have stayed and fought the battle.' He sounded impossibly cynical, and it rankled unbearably.

'I tried.' Dear lord, how she'd tried. But one battle didn't win the war, as she had discovered to her cost. Carly tilted her head at a proud angle. 'Being figuratively savaged by a female predator held no appeal. I much preferred to retreat with dignity.' Her eyes were remarkably clear. 'Besides, it's impossible to lose what you never had.'

'I willingly slid a ring on your finger, and pledged my devotion.' His voice held a soft drawling quality that sent shivers scudding down the length of her spine. 'Was your faith in me so lacking that there was no room for trust?'

The entire conversation had undergone a remarkable change, and she wasn't comfortable with its passage. 'That was a long time ago,' she responded slowly, aware of the tug at her heartstrings, the ecstasy as much as the agony of having loved him. 'Your concept of marriage was different from mine.'

'You're so sure of that?'

A lump rose unbidden in her throat—she doubted her voice could surmount it—and a great weariness settled down on to her young shoulders, making her feel suddenly tired.

'If you don't mind, I'd like to shower and go to bed.'

'Enjoy your solitude, *cara*,' Stefano told her with soft mockery. 'I have a few international calls to make.' His expression was veiled, making it impossible to detect his mood, and she watched as he walked to the door, then he turned towards her.

'Incidentally, I've located a reputable breeder who will deliver Ann-Marie's poodle late tomorrow afternoon.' He paused, a faint smile tugging his lips at her surprise. 'A house-trained young female, black, with impeccable manners, who answers to Françoise. I'll see that I'm home to ensure she has a proper introduction to Prince.'

He opened the door, then closed it quietly behind him before Carly had a chance to say so much as a word.

He was an enigma, she decided as she became caught up in a maelstrom of contrary emotions. There was a sense of unresolved hostility, an inner need that bordered on obsession, to get beneath his skin and test the strength of his anger.

Or his passion, her subconscious mind taunted mercilessly. Wasn't that what she really wanted?

No. The silent scream rose in her throat, threatening, agonising in its intensity, and she gazed sightlessly around the room for several seconds as she attempted to focus on something—anything—that would rationalise her feelings.

All she could see were the two pieces of furniture that totally dominated the large room. Two queensize beds, each expensively quilted in delicately muted matching colours that complemented the suite's elegant furnishings.

A leisurely shower would surely ease some of her emotional tension, she rationalised as she stripped

off her outer clothes, wound the length of her hair
into a knot atop her head, and stepped beneath the
therapeutic warm spray.

Ten minutes later she stood before the mirror clad
in a towelling robe, her hair brushed and confined
into a single braid. Her features were too pale, she
decided, and with a slight shrug she transferred her
gaze to the opulence of her surroundings.

It provided an all too vivid reminder of another
house, in another city, and another time. Then,
she'd followed her heart, so totally enthralled with
the man she had married that every hour apart from
him was an agonising torment.

In those days she'd behaved like a love-crazed
fool, she reflected a trifle grimly. So young, so incredibly naïve, *aching* all day for the evening hours
she could spend in his arms.

Beautiful, soul-shaking hours filled with a lovemaking so incredibly passionate that she would
often wake trembling at the thought that she might
lose him and have it end.

Carly studied her reflection, seeing the subtle
changes seven years had wrought. Her eyes lacked
the luminescent lustre of love, and held an elusive
quality that bore evidence of a maturity gained from
the responsibility of caring emotionally and
financially for herself and her child. Any hint of
naïveté had long since departed, and there was an
inherent strength apparent, an inner determination
to succeed. There was also pain, buried so deep
within her that she rarely allowed it to emerge.

Now she had to fight against the memories that
rose hauntingly to the surface, each one a separate

entity jealously guarded like a rare and precious jewel.

If she closed her eyes she could almost imagine that seven years had never passed, that any moment Stefano would step behind her and slowly, erotically tease her tender nape with a trail of lingering kisses, then gently slide the robe from her shoulders, and extend the physical sense of touching that had begun hours before over dinner with the veiled promise of passion in the depths of those dark eyes. The shared flute of wine; a morsel of food proffered from his plate; the deliberate lingering over coffee and liqueurs, almost as if they were delaying the moment when they'd rise leisurely to their feet and go upstairs to bed.

Even then, they'd rarely hurried, and only once could she recall him being so swept away that he'd lost control, kissing her with such savage hunger that she'd responded in kind, evincing no protest as he'd swiftly slaked his desire. Afterwards he'd enfolded her close in his arms, then he'd made love to her with such exquisite gentleness that she'd been unable to still the soft flow of silent tears.

Carly blinked, then shook her head faintly in an effort to clear away any further treacherous recollection from the past. Yet it wouldn't quite submerge, and she gazed sightlessly into the mirror as she pondered what Stefano's reaction had been when he'd discovered she'd left him.

Good grief! What are you? she demanded of her reflected image. A masochist? He didn't choose to instigate a search to discover your whereabouts, and in all probability he was pleased to be relieved of

a neurotic young wife who warred with him over
his indiscretions.

Damn. The silent curse whispered past her lips,
and with a gesture of disgust she turned off the
light and moved into the bedroom.

There was no purpose to damaging introspection, she resolved as she slid into bed. She was
an adult, and, if he could handle spending the night
hours lying in another bed in the same room, then
so could she.

The challenge was to fall asleep *before* he entered
the bedroom, rather than afterwards, and despite
feeling tired it proved impossible to slip into a state
of somnolent oblivion.

How long she lay awake she had no idea, but it
seemed *hours* before she heard the faint click of the
bedroom door as it unlatched, followed by another
as it was quietly closed.

Every nerve-end tautened to its furthest limit as
she heard the indistinct sound of clothing being
discarded, and she unconsciously held her breath
as she visualised each and every one of his movements, her memory of his tightly muscled naked
frame intensely vivid from the breadth of shoulder
to his slim waist, the whorls of dark hair on his
chest that arrowed down to his navel before feathering in a delicate line to a flaring montage at the
junction of his loins. Firm-muscled buttocks, lean
hips, and an enviable length of strong muscled legs.
Beautiful smooth skin, a warm shield for the blood
that pulsed through his veins and entwined with
honed muscle and sinew.

It was a body she had come to know as inti-
mately as her own as he had tutored her where to

touch, when to brush feather-light strokes that had made him catch his breath, and how the touch of her lips, her tongue, could drive him almost beyond the edge of sensual sanity.

But it had been little in comparison to the response he was able to evoke in her, for all her senses had leapt with fire at his slightest touch, and she had become a willing wanton in his arms, encouraging everything he chose to give, like a wild untamed being in the throes of unbelievable ecstasy. Abandoned, exultant—passion's mistress.

Carly closed her eyes, tight, then slowly opened them again. Dear lord, she must have been insane to imagine she could share this room with him and remain unaffected by his presence.

Was this some form of diabolical revenge he'd deliberately chosen? Did he really intend to *sleep*?

The acute awareness was still there, a haunting pleasurable ache that fired all her senses and ate into her soul. In the past seven years there hadn't been a night when she didn't think of him, and many a time she'd woken shaking at the intensity of her dreaming, almost afraid in those few seconds of regained consciousness that she had somehow regressed into the past. Then she would look at the empty pillow beside her and realise it had all been a relayed figment of her overstimulated imagination.

Several feet separated each bed, yet the distance could have been a yawning chasm ten times that magnitude. Carly heard the almost undetectable sound of the mattress depressing with Stefano's weight as he slid in between the sheets, followed by the slowly decreasing rhythm of his breathing as it steadied into a deep, regular beat denoting total relaxation.

It seemed unbelievable that he could summon sleep so easily, and a seed of anger took root and began to germinate deep within her, feeding on frustration, pain and a gamut of emotions too numerous to delineate.

Rational thought disappeared as her febrile brain pondered the quality of his lovemaking, and whether it would be any different now from what it had been seven years ago.

In that moment she realised how much she was at his mercy, and that the essence of Stefano Alessi the man *now* was inevitably different from the lover she had once known.

At some stage she must have fallen into a blissful state of oblivion, for she gradually drifted into wakefulness through various layers of consciousness, aware initially in those few seconds before comprehension dawned that something was different. Then her lashes slowly flickered open, and she saw why.

In sleep she had turned to lie facing the bed opposite her own, and her eyes widened as she encountered Stefano's steady gaze. Reclining on his side, head propped in one hand, he regarded her with unsmiling appraisal.

Carly's first instinct was to leap out from the bed, and perhaps something in her expression gave her intention away, for one of his eyebrows arched in silent musing cynicism.

The gesture acted as a challenge, and she forced herself to remain where she was. 'What's the time?' she asked with deliberate sleepiness, as if this were just another morning in a series of mornings she woke to find herself sharing a room.

'Early. Not long after six.' His eyes slid lazily down to her mouth, then slipped lower to pause deliberately on the soft swell of her breast. 'No need to rush into starting the day.'

Carly's fingers reached automatically for the edge of the sheet and pulled it higher, aware of a telltale warmth tingeing her cheeks, and her eyes instantly sparked with fire. 'If you think I'm going to indulge in an exchange of pleasantries, you're mistaken!'

'Define *pleasantries*,' Stefano drawled, and she froze, her eyes widening into huge pools of uncertainty in features that had suddenly become pale. There wasn't a shred of softness in his voice, and she was frighteningly aware of her own vulnerability in the face of his superior strength.

'Afraid, Carly?'

'Of a display of raging male hormones?' she managed with a calmness she was far from feeling. He looked dangerous, like a sleek panther contemplating a helpless prey, and it was impossible not to feel apprehensive.

Her lashes flicked wide as his gaze travelled to the base of her throat, then his eyes captured hers with an indolent intensity, and she dredged up all her resources in an attempt to portray some measure of ease.

'Is that all you imagine it will be?' he queried silkily.

'Sex simply to satisfy a base animal need?'

'Cynicism doesn't suit you,' he said in a voice that was deadly soft.

'I've learnt to survive,' she returned with innate dignity. 'Without benefit of anyone other than myself.'

Stefano looked at her for what seemed an age, his gaze dark and inscrutable. 'Until now.'

'Payback time, Stefano?' She forced herself to study him, noting the almost indecently broad shoulders, the firm, sculptured features that embodied an inherent strength of will. 'Are you implying I should slip into your bed and allow you to score the first instalment?'

'With you playing the role of reluctant martyr?' He paused, and his voice hardened slightly. 'I think not, my little cat. I don't feel inclined to give you that satisfaction.'

Her stomach lurched, then appeared to settle. It was only a game, a by-play of words designed to attack her composure. Well, she would prove she was a worthy opponent.

'What a relief to know I don't have to fake it,' she told him sweetly. 'Is there anything else you'd like to discuss before I hit the shower?'

There was lurking humour evident in those dark eyes, and a measure of respect. 'Last week I extended an invitation to Charles and his wife to dine here this evening. They flew in from the States yesterday.'

The thought of having to act the part of gracious hostess in his home, while appearing capable and serene, was a hurdle she wasn't sure she was ready to surmount—yet. However, Charles Winslow the Third was a valued colleague, who, the last time she'd dined in his presence, had been in the throes of divorcing one wife in favour of wedding another.

'What time had you planned for them to arrive?' she queried cautiously, unwilling to commit herself.

'Eight. Sylvana will prepare and serve the meal.'

She had to ask. 'Are they the only guests?'

'Charles's daughter, Georgeanne.'

Seven years ago Georgeanne had been a precocious teenager. Time could only have turned her into a stunning beauty. 'Another conquest, Stefano?' she queried with musing mockery.

'I don't consciously set out to charm every female I come into contact with,' he drawled, and she gave a soundless laugh.

'You don't have to. Your potent brand of sexual chemistry does it for you.'

'An admission, Carly?'

'A statement from one who has sampled a dose and escaped unscathed,' she corrected gravely, and glimpsed the faint edge of humour curve his generous mouth.

'And tonight?'

She looked at him carefully. 'What if I refuse?'

'Out of sheer perversity, or a disinclination to mix and mingle socially?'

'Oh, *both*,' she disclaimed drily. 'I just love the idea of being a subject of conjecture and gossip.'

'Charles is a very good friend of long standing,' Stefano reminded her.

'In that case, I'll endeavour to shine as your hostess,' Carly conceded. 'What of *my* friends?' she pursued.

'Sarah?'

'Yes.' And James. She would mention it when she phoned Sarah this afternoon.

'Feel free to issue an invitation whenever you please.'

Stefano watched with indolent amusement as she slid from the bed, slipped her arms into a towelling wrap, then escaped to the adjoining *en suite*.

Breakfast was a shared meal eaten out on the terrace, after which Stefano withdrew upstairs only to re-emerge ten minutes later, immaculately attired in a dark business suit.

He looked every inch the directorial businessman that he was, and arrestingly physical in a way that set Carly's pulse racing in an accelerated beat. She watched with detached interest as he crossed to the table and brushed gentle fingers to Ann-Marie's cheek.

Somehow she managed to force her features into a stunning smile when his gaze assumed musing indolence as it rested on her mobile mouth.

'Bye. Don't work too hard.' The words sounded light and faintly teasing, but there was nothing light in the glance she spared him beneath dark-fringed lashes.

Minutes later there was the muted sound of a car engine as the Mercedes traversed the long curving driveway.

Ann-Marie's appointment with the neurosurgeon was at ten, and afterwards Carly drove home in a state of suspended shock as she attempted to absorb Ann-Marie's proposed admission into hospital the following day, with surgery scheduled for late Wednesday afternoon.

So *soon*, she agonised, in no doubt that Stefano's influence had added sufficient weight to the surgeon's decision to operate without delay.

It was impossible not to suffer through an entire gamut of emotions, not the least of which was very real fear. Even the neuro-surgeon's assurance that the success-rate for such operations was high did little to alleviate her anxiety.

Stefano arrived home shortly after four, and half an hour later the breeder delivered Françoise—a small, intelligent bundle of black curls who proved to be love on four legs.

The delightful pup took an instant liking to the hulking Prince, who in turn was initially tolerant, then displayed an amusing mixture of bewitchment and bewilderment as Françoise divided her attention equally between him and her new mistress.

There was a new kennel, an inside sleeping-box, leads, a collar, a few soft toys, and feeding bowls.

Ann-Marie looked as if she'd been given the world, and Carly experienced reluctant gratitude for Stefano's timing.

'Thank you,' she said quietly as they emerged from their daughter's bedroom, having settled an ecstatically happy little girl to sleep. Françoise was equally settled in her sleeping-box beside Ann-Marie's bed.

His smile was warm, genuine, she perceived with a slight start of surprise, for there was no evidence of his usual mockery.

'She has waited long enough to enjoy the company of a much wanted pet.'

Carly felt a pang of remorse for the years spent living in rented accommodation which had excluded the ownership of animals. It seemed another peg in the victory stakes for Stefano—a silent comparison of provision. His against hers.

'We have fifteen minutes before Charles is due to arrive,' Stefano intimated as they reached their suite. 'Can you be ready in time?'

She was, with a few seconds to spare, looking attractive in a slim-fitting dress in vivid tones of peacock-green and -blue. Her hair was confined in a simple knot, her make-up understated with practised emphasis on her eyes ... Eyes which met his and held them unflinchingly as she preceded him from the room.

CHAPTER SIX

CHARLES WINSLOW THE THIRD was a friendly, gregarious gentleman whose daughter was of a similar age to his second wife.

If appearances were anything to go by, each young woman had worked hard to outdo the other in the fashion stakes, for each wore a designer label that resembled creations by Dior and Ungaro.

Carly felt her own dress paled by comparison, for although the classic style was elegant it was hardly new.

Within seconds of entering the lounge Charles took hold of Carly's hand and raised it, Southern-style, to his lips.

'I'm delighted the two of you are together again,' he intoned solemnly. 'You're too beautiful to remain unattached, and Stefano was a fool to let you escape.'

Carly caught Stefano's faintly lifted eyebrow and was unable to prevent the slight quiver at the edge of her mouth. Without blinking an eyelid, she sent Charles her most dazzling smile. 'Charles,' she greeted with equal solemnity. 'You haven't changed.'

His faintly wolfish smile was no mean compliment to his sparkling brown eyes. 'My wife tells me I become more irascible with every year, and Georgeanne only tags along because I pay her bills.'

'Ignore him,' Kathy-Lee advised with a light smile.

'Stefano...' Georgeanne purred, offering Carly a sharp assessing glance before focusing her attention on her father's business associate. 'It's wonderful to see you again.'

'Wonderful' was a pretty fine superlative to describe Charles's daughter, Carly mused, for the young woman was all grown up and pure feline.

Kathy-Lee, at least, opted to observe the conventions and set out to charm superficially while choosing to ignore the machinations of her stepdaughter. Which, Carly noted circumspectly, grew more bold with every passing hour. Perhaps it was merely a game, she perceived as they leisurely dispensed with one delectable course after another.

Whatever the reason, Carly refused to rise to the bait, and instead drew Charles into a lengthy and highly technical discourse on the intricacies of computer programming. As he owed much of his fortune to creating specialised programs, his knowledge was unequalled.

Stefano, to give him his due, did nothing to encourage Georgeanne's attention, but Carly detected an implied intimacy that hurt unbearably. It clouded her beautiful eyes, leaving them faintly pensive, and, although her smile flashed with necessary brilliance throughout the evening, her hands betrayed their nervousness on one occasion, incurring Stefano's narrowed glance as she swiftly averted spilling the contents of her wine glass.

Carly told herself she couldn't care less about her husband's past indiscretions, but deep within her resentment flared, and mingled with a certain degree of pain.

Outwardly, Stefano was the perfect host, his attention faultless, and only she knew that the implied intimacy of his smile merely depicted a contrived image for the benefit of their guests.

It was almost eleven when Charles indicated that they must leave.

'It's so early,' Georgeanne protested with a pretty pout. 'I thought we might go on to a nightclub.'

'Honey,' Charles chided with a slow sloping smile before directing Carly a wicked wink, 'I have no doubt Stefano and Carly have a different kind of socialising in mind.'

His daughter effected a faint moue, then sent Stefano a luscious smile. 'Don't be crude, Daddy. I'm sure Stefano has the stamina for both.'

Charles gave Kathy-Lee the sort of look that made Carly's toes curl before switching his attention to his daughter. 'It's no contest, darlin',' he drawled.

Georgeanne evinced her disappointment, then effected a light shrugging gesture. 'If you say so.' She moved a step closer to Stefano and placed scarlet-tipped nails against his jacket-encased arm. *Ciao, caro.*' She reached up and brushed her lips against his cheek—only because he turned his head and she missed his mouth. Her smile was pure celluloid, and there was a faint malicious gleam as she turned towards Carly. 'You look—tired, sweetie.'

Without blinking, Carly met the other girl's sultry stare, and issued softly, 'Stefano doesn't allow me much time to sleep.'

Charles's eyes danced with ill-concealed humour. 'Give it up, Georgeanne.' With old-fashioned charm he took hold of Carly's hand and squeezed it gently. 'You must be our guests for dinner before we fly back to the States.'

Carly simply smiled, and walked at Stefano's side to the foyer. Minutes later Charles, Kathy-Lee and Georgeanne were seated in their hired car, and almost as soon as the rear lights disappeared through the gates Carly moved upstairs to check on Ann-Marie and Françoise.

A tiny black head lifted from the sleeping-box to regard her solemnly, then nestled back against the blanket.

'I'll take her outside for a few minutes, then she should be all right until morning.'

Carly turned slowly at the sound of Stefano's voice, and she nodded in silent acquiescence. Ann-Marie was lost in sleep, her features relaxed and cherubic in the dull reflected glow of her night-light, the covers in place, and her favourite doll and teddy bear vying for affection on either side of her small frame.

Carly felt the sudden prick of tears, and blinked rapidly to dispel them. Her daughter was so small, so dependent—so damned vulnerable.

She was hardly aware of Stefano's return, and it took only seconds to settle the poodle comfortably among its blankets.

Once inside their own suite, Carly stepped directly through to the bathroom and removed her make-up with slightly shaking fingers. Her nerves felt as if they were shredding into a thousand pieces,

and she needed a second attempt at replacing the
lid on the jar of cleanser.

When she re-entered the bedroom Stefano was
propped up in bed, stroking notes into a leather-
bound book, and her stomach executed a series of
flips at his breadth of shoulder, the hard-muscled
chest with its liberal whorls of dark hair tapering
down to a firm waist.

The pale-coloured sheet merely highlighted the
natural olive colour of his skin, and as if sensing
her appraisal he looked up and pinned her gaze,
only to chuckle softly as she quickly averted her
eyes.

'Shy, Carly?' he drawled, and she hated the faint
flood of pink that warmed her cheeks as she moved
towards her bed.

He possessed all the attributes of a superb jungle
animal, resplendent, resting, yet totally focused on
his prey.

An arrow of pain arched up from the centre of
her being in the knowledge that seven years ago she
would have laughed with him, tantalisingly slid the
nightgown from her shoulders—if she'd even opted
to wear one—and walked towards him, sure of his
waiting arms, the rapture that would take them far
into the night.

Now, she fingered the decorative frill on the
pillowslip, and made a play of plumping the pillow,
feeling oddly reluctant to skip into bed, yet longing
for the relaxing effect of several hours' sleep.

'How delightful, *cara*,' Stefano teased mercilessly. 'You can still blush.'

Carly lifted her head and her eyes sparked with
latent fire. 'If you wanted a playmate for the

evening, you should have gone nightclubbing with Georgeanne.'

One eyebrow slanted in silent mockery. 'Why— when I have my very own playmate at home?'

Anger mingled with the fire, and produced a golden-flecked flame within the brilliant darkness of her gaze. 'Because I don't like playing games, and I particularly don't want to play them with *you*!'

'Georgeanne is——'

'I know perfectly well what Georgeanne is!' she vented quietly, hating his level gaze. She was angry, without any clear reason *why*.

'—the daughter of a very good friend of mine,' he continued as if she hadn't spoken, 'who delights in practising her feminine witchery.' His eyes hardened fractionally. 'Charles should have disciplined her precociousness at a young age.'

'Oh—*fiddlesticks*,' Carly responded, unwilling to agree with him. 'Georgeanne suffers from acute boredom, and views any attractive man as a contest. If he's married, that presents even more of a challenge.'

Stefano's eyes speared hers, and his expression assumed a lazy indolence. 'Jealous, *cara*?'

'Stop calling me that!'

'You're expending so much nervous energy,' he drawled imperturbably. 'You'll never be able to relax sufficiently to sleep.'

Without thinking she picked up the pillow and threw it at him, then gasped as he fielded it with one hand and moved with lightning speed to trap her before she had the chance to move. She wrenched her arm in an effort to be free of him, then she cried out as he tightened his grip and pulled her down on to the bed.

There wasn't a chance she could escape, yet to lie quiescent was impossible, and she flailed at him with her free arm, then groaned with despair as he caught it and held her immobile.

His mouth was inches above her own, and she just looked at him, unable to focus her gaze on anything except his strong, chiselled features and the darkness of his eyes.

Time became suspended as she lay still, mesmerised by the look of him, imprisoned in a spellbinding thrall of all her senses. This close, the warmth of his breath skimmed her mouth, and she could smell the faint musky tones of his aftershave, the clean body smell emanating from his skin, and the essential maleness that was his alone. An answering awareness unfurled deep within her, flaring into vibrant life as it coursed through her body with the intensity of flame.

She could see the knowledge of it reflected in his eyes, the waiting expectancy evident as every cell, every nerve-end flowered into a sexual bloom so vivid, so hauntingly warm that she caught his faint intake of breath an instant before his head slowly lowered to claim her mouth in a teasingly gentle kiss that was so incredibly evocative that she was powerless to still the faint prick of tears.

His lips trailed to the sensitive cord at the edge of her neck, nuzzling the sweet hollows, before continuing a slow descent to a highly sensitised nub peaking at her breast.

The anticipation was almost more than she could bear, and she murmured indistinctly, craving the exquisite pleasure of his touch, exulting when he took the tender peak into his mouth and began teasing it with the edge of his teeth.

A deep shooting pain arrowed through her body, and she slid her hands up over his shoulders in a tactile voyage of discovery until her fingers reached the dark curling hair at his nape.

An ache began at the junction of her thighs, and she arched her body against his in unbidden invitation, then she gave a pleasurable sigh as his fingers slid to caress the aroused orifice to a peak of exquisite pleasure, his movements deftly skilled, until nothing less than total possession was enough.

She became mindless, caught in the thrall of a passion so intense that she began to beg, pleading with him in wanton abandon, until with sure movements he plunged deep inside, stilling as she gasped at his level of penetration.

Then slowly he began to withdraw, only to repeat the initial thrust again and again, increasing in rapidity until her body caught hold of his rhythm and then paced it in unison until the momentum tipped them both over the edge into an explosion of ecstasy so tumultuous that she began to shake uncontrollably as the tremors radiated through her body, incandescent, shattering, primitive, the most primal of all the emotions, subsiding gradually to assume a piercing sweetness that stayed with her long after he curled her close in against him and his breathing steadied with her own into the slow, measured pattern of sleep.

*   *   *

Carly retained very little memory of the ensuing few days, for one seemed to run into the other as she spent all her waking hours at the hospital.

'I want to stay with her,' she said quietly to the sister on duty shortly after Ann-Marie was admitted.

'My dear, I understand your concern, but we've found a young child tends to become distraught if the mother rooms in with the child. It really is much more practical if you visit frequently for short periods. Quality time is much better than quantity. Besides,' she continued briskly, 'it allows the medical staff to do their job more efficiently.'

It made sense, but it didn't aid Carly's natural anxiety, for she had hardly slept the night prior to Ann-Marie's surgery, and was a nervous wreck all through the following day, choosing to sit in silent vigil well into the evening, despite being advised to go home and rest.

Stefano came and fetched her, his voice quietly insistent, and she was too mentally and emotionally exhausted to give more than a token protest as he led her out to the car. At home he heated milk, added a strong measure of brandy, and made sure she drank it all.

One day seemed to run into another without Carly having any clear recollection of each, for Ann-Marie was her entire focus from the time of waking until she fell wearily into bed at night.

From Intensive Care, Ann-Marie was released into a suite of her own, and designated a model patient as she began the slow path towards recuperation.

Carly, however, became increasingly tense, for there were still tests to be run, and by the fifth evening she was powerless to prevent the silent flow of tears long after she'd crept into bed.

Reaction, she decided wearily, to all the tension, the anxiety, and insufficient sleep. Yet she couldn't stop, and after a while she slid soundlessly to her feet, gathered up a wrap and walked silently down the hall.

Ann-Marie's bedroom door was closed, and she opened it, her breath catching as she saw the night-light burning and two bright button eyes as Françoise lifted her head to examine the intruder.

A lump rose in her throat as she crossed to the sleeping-box and scooped the curly-haired black bundle into her arms.

The poodle's nose was cool and damp, and Carly hugged her close. A small, wet pink tongue emerged to lick her cheek, then began to lap in earnest at the taste of salty tears. After several long minutes she restored the poodle into its sleeping-box, then slowly crossed to the window.

The curtains were closed, and she opened them fractionally, looking out at the moonlit grounds in detached contemplation.

The small shrubs appeared large with their looming shadows, and everything seemed so still, almost lifeless. Pin-pricks of electric light glittered across the harbour, merging with splashes of flashing neon advertisements gracing several city buildings. By night it resembled a tracery of fairy-lights, remote, yet symbolising activity and pulsing life.

She had no idea how long she remained motionless, for there was no awareness of the passage of time, just a slide into introspection that took her back over six years to the day her daughter was born, and the joy, the tears and the laughter that had followed through a few childhood illnesses, the guilt of having to leave her in child care while she worked, Ann-Marie's first day at kindergarten, her first visit to the zoo, and the day she had started school. She was a quiet, obedient child, but with a mind of her own.

'Unable to sleep?' The query was quietly voiced, and Carly turned slowly to face the man standing in the aperture.

For an age she just looked at him, her eyes large and unblinking in a face that was pale and shadowed, then she turned back to the scene beyond the window. 'I wish it was all over and she was home,' she managed in an emotion-charged voice, and felt rather than heard him move to stand behind her.

'Likewise,' Stefano muttered in agreement.

No power on earth could speed up time, and she closed her eyes in an effort to gain some measure of inner strength. She had to be strong, she *had* to be, she resolved silently.

Hard, muscular arms slid around her waist from behind and pulled her gently back against a solid male frame.

For a moment she resisted, stiffening slightly, then she became prey to the protective shelter he offered, and she relaxed, allowing his strength to flow through her body.

It was like coming home, and the sadness of what they'd once shared, then lost, overwhelmed her. She closed her eyes tightly against the threat of tears, feeling them burn as she fought for control.

For all of a minute she managed to keep them at bay, then they squeezed through to spill in warm rivulets down each cheek to fall one after the other from her chin.

Firm hands slid up to her shoulders and turned her into his embrace, one hand slipping through the thickness of her hair while the other slid to anchor the base of her spine.

It felt so good, so right, so *safe*, and after a long time she slid her hands round his waist, linking them together behind his back.

The strong, measured beat of his heart sounded loud against her ear, and she rested against him for a long time, drawing comfort from his large frame until at last she stirred and began to pull free of him.

Without a word he loosened his hold, and slipping one arm about her waist, he led her back to their suite. Both beds bore evidence of their occupation, and she viewed each, feeling strangely loath to leave the sanctuary of his embrace, yet to go tacitly to his bed would reveal an unspoken willingness for something she was as yet unprepared to give.

For what seemed an age he stood in silence watching the expressive play of emotions chase across her features, then he leant forward and brushed his lips against her cheek, trailing gently up to her temple before tracing slowly down to the edge of her mouth.

It was an evocative caress, his lips gently tracing her own with such a heightened degree of sensitivity, it was almost more than she could bear.

It would be so easy to allow him to continue, to follow a conflagrating path to total possession and its resultant euphoria. Except that it would only be a merging born out of sexual desire, not the meeting of two minds, two souls, the sharing of something so beautiful, so exquisite, that the senses coalesced and became one.

She went still, lowering her hands slowly down to her side, and Stefano lifted his head slightly, viewing the soft mouth, the faint smudges beneath her shimmering eyes, and his expression became watchful, intent, as she sought to swallow the sudden lump that had risen in her throat.

Carly wanted to cry out, yet no sound emerged, and she willed herself to breathe slowly, evenly, as he drew her down on to his bed and pulled her gently into the circle of his arms.

His quietly voiced, 'Sleep easy, *cara*,' sent goose-bumps scudding in numerous directions to places they had no right to invade. She lay there, unable to make so much as a sound, and within minutes she became aware of the steady pattern of his breathing. Then slowly she began to relax, and gradually sheer emotional exhaustion provided a welcome escape into somnolence.

CHAPTER SEVEN

ANN-MARIE continued to improve with each passing day, and there was immense relief at the week's end to receive the neuro-surgeon's voiced confidence of a complete recovery. It balanced the shock of seeing the bandages removed for the first time, and evidence of a vivid surgical scar.

Carly was so elated on leaving the hospital that she decided against phoning Stefano, and opted to tell him the news in person. Consequently it was almost four when she entered the towering modern city block and rode the lift to Reception.

There was a sense of *déjà vu* on stepping into the luxuriously furnished foyer, although this time there was the advantage of needing no introduction. Carly entertained little doubt that an expurgated version of her previous visit had filtered through the office grapevine, and she kept her eyes steady with a friendly smile pinned in place as the receptionist rang through to Stefano's personal secretary.

Renate appeared almost immediately, her features schooled to express warmth and a degree of apologetic charm. 'Stefano is in conference with a colleague,' she enlightened Carly as she ushered her into his private lounge. 'I've let him know you're here, and he said he'll be with you in a matter of minutes.' The smile deepened. 'Can I get you a drink? Coffee? Tea? Something cool?'

'I'd like to use the rest-room first, if I may?'
Carly returned the woman's smile with one of her
own. 'And something cool would be great.'

As she was about to re-enter the lounge several
minutes later a door opened several feet in front of
her to reveal a tall, attractive brunette whose
stunning features were permanently etched in
Carly's mind.

Recognition was instantaneous, and Carly's
whole body went cold as she watched Angelica
Agnelli turn back to the man immediately behind
her and bestow on him a lingering kiss.

Carly felt as if the scene was momentarily frozen
in her brain, like the delayed shutter of a camera,
then the figures began to move, and she watched
as Stefano stood back a pace and let his hands fall
from Angelica's shoulders.

His expression held warm affection, and stabbed
at Carly's heart. At the same moment he lifted his
head, and Carly watched with a sort of detached
fascination as they each became aware of her
presence.

It was rather like viewing a play, she decided as
she glimpsed the darkness in Stefano's eyes an instant before he masked it, and she was prepared to
go on record that the dismay evident in Angelica's
expression was deliberate, for the faint smile of
contrition failed to reach her eyes.

'Carly,' Angelica greeted her with apparent
warmth. 'Stefano told me you were back.' Her expression pooled into one of apparent concern. 'How
is your daughter?'

The faint emphasis on 'your' wasn't missed, and
Carly marshalled innate dignity as a weapon in her

mythical arsenal. 'Ann-Marie is fine, thank you,'
she responded steadily. Her eyes lifted to meet
Stefano's slightly narrowed gaze, and she summoned a deliberately sweet smile. 'Renate is fetching
me a cool drink. I'll wait in the lounge while you
see Angelica out.' She placed imperceptible stress
on the last word, then softened it with a studied
smile as she turned towards the beautifully attired
young woman whose *haute-couture* clothes hugged
a perfect figure. 'Goodbye, Angelica. I'm sure we'll
run into each other again.' Not if I see you first,
she added silently as she turned into the private
lounge.

With extreme care Carly closed the door behind
her, then crossed towards the bar where an iced
pitcher of orange juice stood beside a tall frosted
glass.

Pouring herself a generous measure, she sipped
at it abstractly and told herself she felt no pain.
Dammit, she swore softly. There had to be subvers-
ive psychic elements at play somewhere in the
vicinity, for each time she entered Stefano's private
lounge she was moved to blinding rage.

However, *this* time she'd be calm. Another
voluble, visible display of temper would have the
staff labelling her a shrew. Yet she defied even the
most placid woman not to be driven to anger when
she was faced with evidence of her husband's *af-
faire de coeur*.

It was five minutes before Stefano joined her, and
she turned quietly to face him as he entered the
room. His expression was inscrutable, his eyes
faintly hooded, and he made no attempt at
any explanation.

He looked the epitome of a successful businessman, his three-piece suit dark and impeccably tailored, the pale blue shirt made of the finest silk, and his shoes hand-stitched imported leather.

She was reminded of the saying that 'clothes made the man'. Yet her indomitable husband could have worn torn cut-off jeans and a sweatshirt, and he'd still manage to project a devastating raw virility that had little to do with the physical look of him.

If his relationship with Angelica Agnelli continued to extend beyond that of friends, then anything Carly said would only fuel her own anger and lead inevitably to another confrontation.

Besides, she was twenty-seven, and no longer the naïve, trusting young girl who had believed in one true love. Reality was the knowledge that love didn't conquer all, nor did it always last forever.

'How was Ann-Marie this afternoon?'

Carly met his dark gaze with equanimity. 'Improving,' she informed him steadily. 'The specialist is confident she'll make a full recovery.'

His features relaxed into an expression of immense relief. '*Grazie a Dio*,' he breathed with immense gratitude.

'Obviously it would have been better if I'd phoned with the news.'

One eyebrow slanted above a pair of eyes that had become strangely watchful. 'Why *obviously*?'

'Business, pleasure and personal affairs are an incompatible mix,' she hinted with unaccustomed cynicism, and saw his eyes narrow.

'Angelica——'

'Don't even consider proffering the rather hackneyed explanation that she's merely an associate.' She lifted her chin, and her eyes were remarkably clear as they held his. 'I've heard it all before.'

'Angelica is a valued family friend,' he continued with hard inflexibility, and the gold flecks in her eyes flared with brilliant topaz as she refused to be intimidated in any way.

'*Valued* is a very tame description, Stefano,' Carly responded, wondering what devilish imp was pushing her in a direction she'd sworn not to tread.

'Perhaps you'd care to offer a more lucid alternative,' he drawled with dangerous silkiness, and she was powerless to prevent the surge of anger coursing through her body.

'She wants *you*,' she declared with quiet conviction. 'She always has. For a while I stood in her way. Now that I'm back . . .' She trailed off deliberately, then effected a slight shrug. 'If she can hurt me emotionally, she will.' The need to be free of him was paramount, and she turned to leave, only to have a detaining hand catch hold of her arm and pull her back to face him.

Any escape could only be temporary. It was there in his eyes, the latent anger a silent threat should she continue to thwart him.

'Let me go.' The words left her throat as his head lowered, and she turned slightly so that his lips grazed her cheek. Then she cried out as he slid his fingers through the thickness of her hair, and his mouth captured hers in a kiss that was nothing less than a total possession of her senses.

A muffled groan of entreaty choked in her throat as he brought her even closer against his hard, muscular frame, and when he finally lifted his head she stood quite still, bearing his silent scrutiny until every nerve stretched to its furthest limit.

His hands slid with seductive slowness to her waist, then cradled her ribcage, the pads of each thumb beginning an evocative circle over the hardening peaks of her breasts in a movement that was intensely erotic.

She had to stop him *now*, before she lost the will to move away. 'Sex in the office, Stefano? Whatever will Renate think?' she taunted softly. 'Or maybe she's accustomed to her boss's...discreet diversions?'

His eyes narrowed, and a muscle hardened at the edge of his jaw. 'Watch your foolish tongue.'

Carly laughed, a soft mocking sound that was the antithesis of anything related to humour. Gathering courage, she added with unaccustomed cynicism, 'I imagine many women shared your table as well as your bed in the last seven years.'

His eyes stilled for a second, then assumed a brooding mockery. 'You want me to supply a list, *cara*?'

For one heart-stopping moment she looked stricken. The thought of that long, superbly muscled body giving even one other woman the sort of sexual pleasure he gave her was sickening. To consider there had probably been *several* made her feel positively ill. Suddenly she'd had enough, and was in dire need of some breathing space—preferably as far away from her inimical husband as possible.

If she didn't leave soon, the ache behind her eyes would result in silent futile tears, and without a further word she turned and left the room.

Within minutes of reaching home she crossed to the phone and dialled Sarah's number. At the sound of her friend's voice she clutched hold of the receiver and sank down into a nearby chair for a long conversation that encompassed an exchange of news as well as providing a link to normality.

'You must bring James to dinner,' Carly insisted as Sarah exclaimed at the time. 'I'll check with Stefano and give you a call.'

'Lovely,' the other girl declared with enthusiasm. 'Give Ann-Marie a big hug from me, and tell her I'll visit tomorrow.'

Dinner was a strained meal, for Carly found it difficult to contribute much by way of conversation that didn't come out sounding horribly banal. In the end, she simply gave up, and pushed her food around the plate before discarding her cutlery to sip iced water from her glass.

Stefano, damn him, didn't appear a whit disturbed, and he did justice to the dishes Sylvana provided before finishing with fresh grapes, biscuits and cheese.

Carly sat in silence during the drive to hospital, unwilling to offer so much as a word in case it ended in a slanging match—or worse.

There was such a wealth of resentment at having witnessed the touching little departure scene between Angelica and Stefano that afternoon—and unabating anger. It almost eclipsed the joy of witnessing Ann-Marie's pleasure in their visit, and the

expressive smile when Stefano presented her with
yet another gift.

'I'm getting spoilt,' Ann-Marie concluded,
hugging the beautifully dressed doll close to her
small chest, and her eyes gleamed when her father
leaned down to brush his lips against her cheek.
'Thank you, Daddy.'

The words held such poignancy that Carly had
to blink fast against the threat of tears.

'My pleasure, *piccina*.'

'What's a *piccina*?'

'A special endearment for a special little girl,' he
responded gently.

It was almost eight when the Mercedes pulled into
the driveway leading to Stefano's elegant home, and
once indoors Carly made her way through to the
kitchen.

'Coffee?' It was a perfunctory query that incurred his narrowed gaze.

'Please.'

Her movements were automatic as she filled the
percolator, selected a fresh filter, then spooned in
a blend of ground coffee-beans.

'Would you prefer yours here, or in the lounge?'

'The lounge.'

Damn, that meant she'd have to share it with him,
yet if she opted out he'd only be amused, and she
refused to give him the satisfaction.

Five minutes later she placed cups and saucers,
sugar and milk on to a tray and carried it through
to the informal lounge. Placing his within easy
reach, she selected a chair several feet distant from
where he was seated.

'We've been invited out to dinner tomorrow evening,' Stefano informed her with indolent ease as he spooned in sugar and stirred the thick black liquid in his cup. 'Charles Winslow will be there with Kathy-Lee.' His eyes seared hers, darkly analytical in a manner that raised all her fine body hairs in a gesture of self-defence.

'And Georgeanne?' She arched a brow in deliberate query. 'I'm not sure I want to go.' The thought of standing at his side for several hours playing a part didn't figure very high in her order of preferred entertainment.

'Most of the men present will have their wives or partners in attendance,' he drawled, and she said sweetly,

'Why not invite Angelica? I'm sure she'd delight in the opportunity. Then you could have two women vying for your attention.'

One eyebrow slanted in quizzical mockery, although anything approaching humour was sadly lacking in his expression. 'I'll ignore that remark.'

A crazy imp prompted her to query, 'Good heavens, *why*? It's nothing less than the truth.'

His expression didn't alter. 'Watch your unwary tongue, *mi moglie*,' he cautioned in a deadly soft voice.

'Don't threaten me,' she responded swiftly, feeling the deep-rooted anger begin to surge to the surface.

'Warn,' he amended with quiet emphasis.

'There's a difference?'

His eyes lanced hers, silent and deadly in their intent. 'Give it up, Carly.'

'And concede defeat?'

'If you want to fight,' Stefano drawled with dangerous silkiness, 'I'm willing to oblige.' He paused deliberately, then continued, 'I doubt you'll enjoy the consequences.'

A shaft of exquisite pain arrowed through her body, although defiance was responsible for the angry tilt of her chin as she berated, 'I seem to remember you preferred your women warm and willing.'

'What makes you think you won't be, *cara*?' Stefano drawled, his expression veiled as pain clouded her beautiful eyes, rendering her features hauntingly vulnerable for a few heart-stopping seconds before the mask slipped into place.

She was treading dangerous waters, yet she was too incensed to desist. 'Did it never occur to you that my taste in men may have changed?'

'Have there been that many?' His voice sounded like finely tempered steel grazing satin, and she had the incredible desire to shock.

'Oh—*several*.'

Something leapt in the depth of his eyes, and she wanted to cry out a denial, yet the words remained locked in her throat.

What on earth was the matter with her in taunting him? Playing any kind of game with a man of Stefano's calibre was akin to prodding a sleeping jungle animal.

'I had a life during the past seven years, Stefano,' she flung, more angry than she'd care to admit. 'Didn't you?'

'Do you really want to pursue this topic?'

'Why?'

'Because it will have only one ending,' he warned with incredible silkiness, although his eyes were hard and obdurate, and there could be no doubt as to his meaning.

'Go to hell,' she whispered, hating him more at that precise moment than she'd thought it possible to hate anyone.

The need to get away from him was paramount, and, uncaring of his reaction, she turned and walked out of the room, out of the house, moving with a quick measured pace along the driveway to the electronically locked steel gates.

For the first time she damned Stefano's security measures as logic and sanity temporarily vanished in the face of a fierce, unbating anger.

The house, the grounds, were like an impenetrable fortress, necessary in today's age among the exceedingly wealthy in a bid to protect themselves, their family and their possessions.

She could return indoors, collect her keys and the necessary remote module to release the main gates, but even in anger sufficient common sense exerted itself to warn silently against walking the suburban streets alone after dark. And if she took her car, where would she go? It was too late for visiting, and Sarah, if she wasn't working, would probably be out with James.

Carly turned back towards the house and slowly retraced her steps. The air was warm, with the faintest breeze teasing a few stray tendrils of her hair, and she lifted her face slightly, looking deep into the indigo sky with its nebulous moon and sprinkling of stars.

Drawing in a deep breath, she released it slowly. A strange restlessness besieged her, and she felt the need for some form of exercise to help expel her pent-up emotions.

There was a pool in the rear of the grounds, and she instinctively took the path that skirted the southern side of the house.

Reflected light from several electric lamps strategically placed in the adjacent rockery garden lent the pool a shimmering translucence, and, without giving too much thought to her actions, Carly stripped off her outer clothes and executed a neat dive into the pool's clear depths. Within seconds she was cleaving clean strokes through the cool water, silently counting as she completed each length. After twenty-five she rested for a few minutes, clearing the excess water from her face, her hair.

'Had enough?'

Carly lifted her head and looked at the tall figure standing close to the pool's edge. In the subdued light he loomed large, his height and breadth magnified by reflected shadows.

'Is there some reason why I shouldn't take advantage of the pool?'

'None whatsoever,' Stefano declared mockingly. 'Shall I help you out?' At his drawled query she raised a hand, then when he grasped it she tugged *hard*, experiencing a thrill of exultation as he lost his balance and was unable to prevent a headlong fall into the water.

Fear of retaliation lent wings to her limbs as she levered herself up on to the pool's edge, then, scooping up her clothes, she sped quickly into the house.

A faint bubble of laughter emerged from her throat as she entered the bedroom. She'd have given almost anything to glimpse the expression on his face!

Moving straight through to the adjoining bathroom, she turned on the shower, discarded her briefs and bra, then stepped beneath the warm, pulsing water.

Selecting shampoo, she massaged it through the length of her hair, then rinsed it off before reaching for the soap—and encountered a strong male hand.

'Is this what you're looking for?'

She went still with shock as fear unfurled in the region of her stomach. Slowly she pushed back the wet length of her hair, and a silent gasp parted her lips at the sight of him standing within touching distance, every last vestige of clothing removed from his powerful frame.

'Ready to cry wolf, Carly?'

No sooner had the soft taunt left his lips than she felt the soap sweep in a tantalisingly slow arc from the tip of her shoulder to the curve at her waist. She had to get out *now*. She tried, except that one hand closed over her arm, holding her still, while the other curved round her shoulder, and she was powerless to resist as he turned her round to face him.

'I'm sorry.' It was a half-hearted apology, and his answering smile was wholly cynical as his fingers trailed an evocative path over the surface of her skin, tracing the delicate line of her collarbone, then brushing lower to the dark aureole surrounding the tight bud of her left breast.

'Don't.' The single plea went unheeded, and her stomach quivered as his hand slid to caress her hip, the narrow indented waist, before traversing to cup the soft roundness of her bottom.

Without her being aware of it, he'd managed to manoeuvre her so that the jet of water streamed against his back, and she stood still, her eyes wide and luminous beneath his hooded gaze.

'Stefano——' she protested as he pulled her close against him. His arousal was a potent virile force, and she arched back, straining against the circle of his arms in an effort to put some distance between them.

'You can't do this,' she whispered in a broken voice.

Yet he could, very easily. He knew it, just as she did. All it would take was one long drugging open-mouthed kiss to destroy any vestige of her self-restraint.

One strong hand slid up to cup her nape, his thumb tilting the uppermost edge of her jaw, holding it fast as she attempted to twist her head away from him. Then his lips brushed hers, lightly at first, teasing, nibbling, tasting in a manner that was deliberately erotic, and left her aching with a terrible hunger, that longing for the satisfaction only he could give.

She resisted for what seemed a lifetime, but playing cool to Stefano's undoubted expertise wreaked havoc with her nervous system, and she gave a hollow groan of despair as he lifted her high up against him, parting her thighs so that she straddled his waist, then she cried out as he lowered his head and took one tender peak into his mouth, suckling with such flagrant eroticism that she clutched hold of his hair in an effort to have him desist.

Just when she thought she could stand it no longer, he transferred his attention and rendered a similar attention to its twin until she begged him to stop.

Then he slowly raised his head, his eyes incredibly dark as they speared hers, and she felt her lips tremble uncontrollably at the sense of purpose evident. Time became a suspended entity, and she couldn't have torn her gaze away if her life depended on it.

With a sense of impending fascination she watched in mesmerised silence as his mouth lowered down over her own, and she gave a silent gasp as he plundered the moist cavern at will, punishing, tantalising, until she gave the response he sought.

When at last he lifted his head she wanted to weep, and she just looked at him, her soft mouth quivering and faintly bruised as she blinked rapidly against the rush of warm tears.

As soon as his hands curved beneath her bottom she knew what he meant to do, and she swallowed convulsively.

His entry was slow, stretching silken tissues to their furthest limit as they gradually accepted his swollen length, and his eyes trapped hers, witnessing her every expression as he carefully traversed the tight, satiny tunnel leading to the central core of her femininity.

Her beautiful eyes widened measurably as his muscular shaft attained its pinnacle. The feeling of total enclosure was intense, and a slow warmth gradually flooded her being, radiating in a tumultuous tide until her whole body was consumed with it. The blood vessels swelled and became engorged, activating muscle spasms over which she had no control, and she unconsciously clenched her thighs, instinctively arching away from him as a pulsating rhythm took her towards fulfilment.

At the zenith, she threw back her head, gasping as he drew her close and feasted shamelessly at her breast, tossing her so close to the edge between pain and pleasure that the two became intermingled, and she cried out, caught in the sweet torture of sexual ecstasy.

Then his hands shifted to her hips, lifting her slightly as he began a slow, tantalising circular movement that sent her to the brink and beyond before he took his pleasure with deep driving thrusts that drew soft guttural cries of encouragement which she refused to recognise as her own.

Afterwards he held her close for what seemed an age, then he gently withdrew and lowered her carefully to her feet.

She stumbled slightly, and clutched hold of him, then she stood transfixed as he caught up the soap and slowly cleansed every inch of her body.

When he'd finished he held out the bar of soap and when she shook her head he placed it in her palm before covering it with his own and transferring it to his chest. His eyes never left hers as he carefully traversed every ridge, every muscle, until his ablutions were complete.

She ached, everywhere. Inside and out. And she stood quiescent as he gently towelled her dry, then transferred his attention to removing the moisture from his own body.

Carly felt totally enervated, and she was powerless to resist as he placed a thumb and forefinger beneath her chin. She wanted to cry, and there were tears shimmering, welling from the depth of her eyes. There was a deep sense of emotional loss for the passion of mind and spirit they'd once shared. For then it had been a joy, a total merging of all the senses, transcending everything she'd ever dreamed ... and more.

Her lashes fluttered down, veiling her expression, and concealing the haunting vulnerability she knew to be evident.

Without a word he slid an arm beneath her knees and carried her through to the bedroom, sweeping back the covers on the bed before slipping with her beneath the sheets.

Carly craved the sweet oblivion of sleep, but it had never seemed more distant, and she provided little resistance as Stefano curved her close in against him. She felt his lips brush the top of her head, and the gentle caress of his hand as it stroked the length of her body before coming to rest on the soft silken curls at the junction between her thighs. His fingers made a light probing foray, and she stiffened as they encountered the slight ridge caused by endless sutures.

'You had a difficult birth with Ann-Marie?'

Carly closed her eyes, then opened them again. 'Yes,' she acknowledged quietly, and felt silent anger emanate through his powerful body as he swore softly, viciously, in his own language. There was no point informing him that her meagre savings hadn't allowed for the luxury of private care.

Nor, in the long silent minutes that slowly ticked by, could she assure him that the wonder of holding Ann-Marie in her arms for the first time swept aside the trauma of a painful birth.

Even now it was a vivid memory, and she stared sightlessly into the darkness as she recalled the joy and the tears associated with those initial few years as she'd struggled to support them both.

Carly became aware of the soft brush of his fingers against her skin, and felt the faint stirring deep within her as her body responded to his touch. She wanted to move away, but she was caught in a mystical mesmeric spell, and she gave a faint despairing moan as his lips sought the soft hollows at the base of her throat in an erotic savouring that sent the blood coursing through her veins like quicksilver.

Not content, he trailed a path to her breasts to begin an evocative tasting that made her arch against him, and she barely registered the faint guttural sounds that whispered into the night air as his mouth travelled lower, teasing, tantalising, until she was driven almost mad with need.

When he reached the most intimate crevice of all she cried out at the degree of pleasure he was able to arouse, until ecstasy transcended mere pleasure, and she begged, pleading with him to ease the ache deep within her. Yet he stilled her limbs, soothing her gently as he brought her to a climax so tumultuous that it was beyond any mortal description, then he took her in his arms and rolled on to his back, carrying her with him so that she straddled his hips, his mouth warm as he pulled her head down to hers in a kiss so sweetly passionate that she almost cried.

His mouth left hers and trailed to nuzzle the sweet hollows at the base of her throat, then he shifted his hands to her ribcage as he gently positioned her, his eyes dark and intently watchful of the play of emotions chasing across her expressive features as she accepted his full length.

Carly felt a heady sense of power, and her eyes widened slightly as she glimpsed the slumberous passion evident in his dark eyes, the gleam of immense satisfaction, and knew the measure of his control. Unconsciously she arched her body, stretching like a playful young kitten, and revelled at his immediate response.

'Careful, *cara*,' he bade teasingly. 'Or you may get more than you bargained for.'

She moved against him with slow deliberation, undulating her hips in a gentle erotic movement that drew a warning growl, then his hands closed over her lower waist, and she lost control as he set the pace, taking her higher and higher until she cried out and clung on to his arms in a bid to gain some balance in an erotic ride that had no equal. At least, not in her experience.

Slowly, gradually, his movements began to ease, and then his hands slid to her hips, holding her still as he gently stroked his length, almost withdrawing before plunging with infinite slowness until she felt a wondrous suffusing of heat that swelled, triggering a miasma of sensation spiralling through her body until every nerve-end seemed to radiate with exquisite sweetness.

He shuddered, his large body racked with emotion, and she looked at him with an incredible sense of wonder as he became caught in the throes of passion: man at his most vulnerable, adrift in a swirling vortex of sexual experience.

Then his breathing began to slow, and the madly beating pulse at his throat settled into a steady beat. His features softened and his eyes became luminescent for a few heart-stopping minutes, and just for a milli-second she glimpsed the heart of his soul.

Then his hands slid up to cup her breasts, caressing with such acute sensitivity that she caught her breath, and she made no demur as he gently drew her down to him, cradling her head against a muscled shoulder. His fingers trailed over her hair, while a hand slid with tactile softness down the length of her spine. She felt his lips brush across her forehead, then settle at her temple, soothing, until the shivery warm sensation gradually diminished and she was filled with a dull, pleasurable ache.

'I hurt you.' The words held a degree of regretful remorse, and she stirred faintly against him.

Tomorrow there would be an unaccustomed tenderness evident, but she didn't care, for it had nothing to do with physical pain, merely satiated pleasure in its most exhilarating extreme. She sought to reassure him, and moved her lips against his throat, then gently nipped a vulnerable hollow.

'You still want to play?' His voice reverberated against her mouth, and she felt rather than heard his soft husky laughter when she shook her head in silent negation.

'Then go to sleep, *cara bella*,' Stefano bade her gently.

And she did, drifting easily into dreamless oblivion, unaware that he carefully disengaged her and curled her into the curve of his body before reaching for the sheet to cover their nakedness.

CHAPTER EIGHT

CARLY put the final touches to her hair, then stood back and surveyed her reflection. The deep jacaranda-blue gown was classically styled, comprising a figure-hugging skirt and a camisole top with twin shoestring straps that emphasised her slim curves and pale honey-gold skin. Make-up was understated, with emphasis on her eyes, and a clear peach lipstick coloured her generous mouth. Her only jewellery was a slim gold chain at her neck and small gold hoops at her ears. With the length of her hair confined in an elaborate knot atop her head, she looked ... passable, she decided. Or at least able to feel sufficiently confident among guests at a dinner to be held in one of Stefano's business associate's home in nearby Seaforth.

'Stunning,' a deep voice drawled, and she turned slowly to see Stefano standing a few feet distant, looking the epitome of sophistication in an impeccably tailored dark suit, white silk shirt and dark silk tie.

Carly proffered a slight smile and let her eyes slide to a point just beyond his left shoulder. 'Thank you.' Turning, she collected a black beaded evening bag, slipped in a lipstick and compact, then drew in a deep breath as she preceded him from the room to the head of the staircase.

Several minutes later she was seated in the Mercedes as it purred down the driveway towards the street.

When they reached the hospital Ann-Marie was sitting up in bed, together with the doll Stefano had given her, a favoured book, and a teddy bear slightly the worse for wear from which she refused to be parted because, she assured her mother, he was as old as she was, and watched over her as she slept.

She looked, Carly decided with maternal love, as bright as a proverbial button, although there were still slight smudges beneath the beautiful dark eyes, and her skin was transparently pale—visible effects of the aftermath of extensive surgery, the specialist had assured.

Soon she would be able to come home. By the start of the new school year in February, she would be able to resume her classes. Except for the short curly hair, no one would ever know she'd undergone extensive neuro-surgery.

Stefano was wonderful with her, gently teasing, warm, ensuring that Ann-Marie's initial wariness was a thing of the past.

'You look tired, Mummy. Didn't you sleep well last night?'

The words brought a faint smile to Carly's lips. Out of the mouths of babes! 'I stayed up too late,' she relayed gently. 'And woke early.' Was woken up, she amended silently, and persuaded to share a spa-bath, then put back into bed and brought fresh orange juice, toast and coffee on a tray.

'You should rest, like me,' Ann-Marie advised with the ingenuousness of the very young, and Stefano lifted a hand to ruffle her curls.

'I shall ensure she does.'

It was eight when they left, and Carly turned slightly towards him as he eased the car on to the main road.

'How many people will be there tonight?' Her features assumed a faint pensive expression. 'Perhaps you should fill me in with a few background details of key associates.'

'Relax, Carly. This is mainly a social occasion.'

'Yet the men will inevitably gravitate together and discuss business,' she said a trifle drily, and incurred a long probing look as he paused through an intersection.

'Nervous?'

'Should I be?' she countered with remarkable steadiness, considering the faint fluttering of butterfly wings already apparent in her stomach.

'I have no doubt you'll cope admirably.'

She sat in silence during the drive, and glanced out of the window with interest as he turned the Mercedes into a suburban street bordered on each side by tall, wide-branched trees. Seconds later the car turned into a curved driveway lined with late-model cars.

The butterflies in her stomach set up an increasing beat as she slid out from the passenger seat and moved to his side, unprepared within seconds to have him thread his fingers through hers as they walked towards the main entrance. The pressure of his clasp was light, yet she had the distinct feeling he wouldn't allow her to pull free from him.

They were almost the last to arrive, and after a series of introductions Carly accepted a glass of mineral water and attempted to relax.

It wasn't a large group, sixteen at most, she decided as she cast a circumspect glance around the elegantly furnished lounge.

Stefano possessed a magnetic attraction that wasn't contrived, and Carly couldn't help but be aware of the attention he drew from most of the women present.

Seven years ago she'd lacked essential *savoir-faire* to cope with the socially élite among Stefano', fellow associates. Nervous and unsure of herself, she'd chosen to cling to his side and smile, whereas now she was well able to stand on her own feet. It had to make a difference in her ability to cope with his lifestyle.

Canapés and hors-d'oeuvres were proffered at intervals over the next half-hour, and it was almost nine when Charles and Kathy-Lee Winslow arrived with Georgeanne.

'We were held up,' Charles declared with droll humour as he steered his wife to where Carly stood at Stefano's side.

'By a taxi driver who decided to take advantage of the obvious fact we weren't residents, and drove us via a few scenic routes that lost us twenty minutes and gained him twenty extra dollars,' Georgeanne declared in explanation.

'Stop complaining,' Charles chastised with a broad smile. 'We enjoyed a pleasant ride, we're here, and I doubt anyone has missed us.'

'I need a drink,' his daughter vowed, her eyes settling deliberately on Stefano. 'Would you mind?'

The smile she bestowed was nothing short of total bewitchment. 'I'm thirsty.'

Not just for a drink, Carly surmised wryly, for Georgeanne's behaviour fell just short of being blatant, and she watched with faint bemusement as Stefano elicited Georgeanne's preference.

'Why, there's Angelica,' Charles's daughter announced, and her eyes flew towards Carly with a very good imitation of expressed concern. 'Oh, dear, how—awkward.'

This could, Carly decided, become one of those evenings where Murphy's Law prevailed, and she wondered what on earth she could have done to upset some mythical evil spirit who clearly felt impelled to provide her with such an emotional minefield.

With detached fascination she watched Angelica locate Stefano's tall frame at the bar, then cross leisurely to join him. She saw the beautiful brunette lift a manicured hand and touch his arm, saw him turn, and caught his smile in greeting. Angelica's expression was revealingly warm. *Loving*, Carly added, feeling as if she'd just been kicked in the stomach.

A confrontation was inevitable, and when they were seated for dinner Carly cursed the unkind hand of fate as she saw Georgeanne opposite at the large dining-table, with Angelica slightly to Georgeanne's right.

Wonderful, she groaned silently as she sipped a small quantity of white wine in the hope that it would provide a measure of necessary courage with which to get through the evening.

Their hosts provided a sumptuous meal comprising no fewer than five courses if one counted the fresh fruit and cheeseboard that followed dessert. The presentation of the food was impressive, and Carly dutifully forked morsels into her mouth without tasting a thing.

Conversation flowed, and she was aware of an increasing tension as she waited for the moment Angelica would unsheathe her claws.

'How is *your* daughter?'

Again, the faint emphasis didn't go unnoticed, and Carly turned slightly to meet the brunette's seemingly innocent gaze as she summoned a polite smile. 'Ann-Marie is improving steadily.' She aimed for a subtle emphasis of her own. '*We're* hopeful it won't be long before she's released from hospital.'

Angelica picked up her wine glass and fingered the long crystal stem with studied deliberation. 'Stefano appears to delight in playing the role of devoted *Papà*.'

Carly effected a negligible shrug. 'You, more than anyone, should appreciate that Italian men are renowned for their love of family.'

Carefully shaped eyebrows rose a fraction in unison with the faint moue of evinced surprise that was quickly camouflaged with a smile. 'Proud of their sons, protective of their daughters.'

Carly couldn't resist the dig. 'And their wives.'

'Well, of course.' The voice resembled a husky purr, infinitely feline. 'And their mistresses.' Her eyes assumed a warm intimacy that was deliberate 'What female of any age could resist Stefano?'

Carly felt like screaming, but she forced her mouth to curve into a soft smile, and her beautiful eyes assumed a misty expression that was deliberately contrived as she lifted her shoulders in a helpless shrugging gesture that she tempered with a light musing laugh. 'None, I imagine.'

Stefano, damn him, was seemingly engrossed in conversation with Charles, and appeared oblivious to the content of her conversation with Angelica.

What on earth did he imagine they had to discuss, for heaven's sake? The weather? The state of the nation?

It seemed forever before their host suggested adjourning to the lounge for coffee, and she felt strangely vulnerable as the men gravitated together on the pretext of sharing an after-dinner port while the women sought comfortable chairs at the opposite end of the large room—with the exception of Angelica, who stood at Stefano's side, a blatant disparity among men, yet totally at ease with their conversation. It was carrying feminism and equality among the sexes a little too far, surely? Carly couldn't help wondering if the men felt entirely comfortable. Yet she knew Angelica didn't give a fig what her male colleagues thought. Her main motivation in joining the men was to clarify the contrast between two women—herself and Stefano's wife.

The difference was quite marked in every way, from physical appearance to business qualifications. Seven years ago it had seemed important, the chasm too wide for Carly to imagine she would ever bridge. Except that in her own way she had, for there was now a diploma, experience and added qualifications in her field, as well as respect from her peers. There wasn't a thing she needed to prove,

and if she so chose she could join Stefano's associ
ates and discuss any topic relating to corporate ac
counting and tax legislation.

The coffee was liquid ambrosia, and Carly sipped
it appreciatively, wondering just how long it would
be before they left.

'You must visit when Stefano brings you to the
states.'

Carly smiled, then thanked Charles's wife for the
invitation. 'It's quite a few years since I was last
there.'

'The house is large,' Kathy-Lee pursued. 'We'd
be delighted if you'd stay. We love having guests.'

Carly could only admire Kathy-Lee for keeping
pace with Charles's high-flying existence, *and*
playing stepmother—a masterly feat in keeping the
peace, for Charles adored his precocious daughter.

'I'll leave the decision to Stefano,' she said gently,
indulging in inconsequential conversation for
almost thirty minutes before Kathy-Lee had her cup
refilled and was drawn by their hostess to join
another guest who had professed an interest in
Kathy-Lee's preoccupation with interior design.

Carly let her gaze wander round the room, set
tling on the broad frame of her husband as he stood
idolently at ease and deep in conversation with two
of his associates—one of whom was Angelica.

Carly forced herself to study them with impartial
eyes—difficult when she wanted physically to tear
Stefano and Angelica apart.

Angelica was a seductive temptress beneath the
designer gown, leaning imperceptibly toward
Stefano, her eyes, hands, *body* receptive to the man
at her side, whereas Stefano stood totally at ease

his stance relaying relaxed confidence, an assurance that wasn't contrived. And, try as she might, Carly could find no visible sign of any implied intimacy—on his part.

Almost as if he was aware of her scrutiny, he turned slightly and met her gaze. For a moment everything else faded into obscurity, and she watched in bemused fascination as he excused himself and crossed the room to settle his length comfortably on the padded arm of her chair.

His proximity put her at an immediate disadvantage, for she was extremely aware of the clean smell of his clothes, the faint aroma of soap intermingling with his chosen aftershave, an exclusive mixture of spices combined with muted musk that seemed to heighten the essence of the man himself.

Within minutes his associates followed his actions in joining their wives, and Carly wasn't sure which she preferred... being alone with a clutch of curious women, or having to contend with Stefano's calculated attention.

'Almost ready to leave, *cara*?'

His voice was a soft caress, and if anyone was in any doubt as to his affection for his wife he lifted a hand and swept back a swath of curls that had fallen forward, letting his fingers rest far too long at the edge of her throat.

There was a degree of deliberation in his movement, almost as if he was attempting to set a precedent, and it made her unaccountably angry.

She wanted to move away, yet such an action was impossible, and it took all her acting ability to sit still as he brushed gentle fingers across her collarbone then slid them down her arm to thread through

her own. The look in his eyes was explicitly se
ducing, and to any interested observer it was only
too apparent that he couldn't wait to get her home
and into bed.

Well, two could play at that game, and she gently
dug the tips of her nails into the tendons of his
hand, then pressed *hard*. 'Whenever you are,' she
acquiesced lightly, casting him a soft winsome smile
that was deceptively false. She would have liked to
kill him, or at least render some measure of physical
harm, yet in a room full of people she could only
smile. As soon as they were alone, she'd verbally
slay him.

He knew, for his eyes assumed a mocking gleam
that hid latent amusement, almost in silent accept
ance of an imminent battle.

With an indolent movement he rose to his feet
and Carly followed his actions, adding her appreci
ation with genuine politeness as they thanked their
hosts and bade Charles and Kathy-Lee goodbye.

'So early, Stefano?' Angelica queried, effectively
masking her displeasure.

'My wife is tired.'

It was nothing less than the truth, but she re
sented the implication.

Angelica's eyes narrowed, then assumed specu
lative amusement as she proffered Carly a com
miserating smile. 'Can't stand the pace?'

'Quite the contrary,' Carly demurred sweetly.
'Stefano is merely providing a clichéd excuse.'

The resentment was simmering just beneath the
surface of her control, and she contained it until
the Mercedes had swept from the driveway.

'You enjoyed setting me among the pigeons, didn't you?' she demanded in a low, furious tone.

'Was it so bad?'

To be honest, it hadn't been. Yet she was loath to agree with him—on anything. 'On a scale of one to ten in the curiosity stakes, our reconciliation has to rate at least a nine,' she declared drily as he sent the opulent vehicle speeding smoothly through the darkened streets.

'You more than held your own, *cara*,' he said with drawled humour.

Inside she felt like screaming, aware that it would take several weeks before the speculative looks, the gossip abated and eventually died. In the meantime she had to run the gauntlet, and she felt uncommonly resentful.

'Nothing has changed,' Carly voiced with a trace of bitterness, and incurred his swift scrutiny.

'In what respect?'

'You have to be *kidding*,' she declared vengefully. 'Angelica would have liked to eat you alive.' She was so incensed that she wasn't aware of the passion evident in her voice, or the pain.

Turning her attention to the darkened city streets, she watched the numerous vehicles traversing the well-defined lanes with a detached fascination. The bright neon signs provided a brilliant splash of colour that vied with the red amber and green of traffic-lights controlling each intersection.

Transferring her attention beyond the windscreen, she looked sightlessly into the night, aware that Stefano handled the car with the skilled ease of long practice.

The same ease with which he handled a woman: knowledgeable, experienced, and always one step ahead. Just once she'd like to be able to best him, catch him off guard.

Yet even as the resentment festered she knew instinctively that he'd never allow her to win. A solitary battle, possibly, in their ongoing private war, as a musing concession to her feminine beliefs. But never the war itself.

It was twenty minutes before the Mercedes drew to a halt inside the garage, and Carly made her way upstairs to the main suite.

She was in the process of removing her make-up when Stefano entered the room, and her eyes assumed a faint wariness as she completed the task.

It required only a few steps to move into the bedroom, a few more to reach the bed. Yet she was loath to take them, knowing what awaited her once she slipped between the cool percale sheets.

Fool she derided silently. It's not as if you lack enjoyment in the marital bed.

The knowledge of her exultant abandon in Stefano's arms merely strengthened her resolve to provide delaying tactics, and she plucked the pin from the elaborate knot restraining her hair, only to catch hold of her brush and stroke it vigorously through the length of tumbled auburn-streaked curls.

It was mad to want more, insane to build an emotional wall between them. A tiny logical voice rationalised that she should be content. She had a beautiful home, and a husband whose business interests ensured they were among the denizens of the upper social echelon.

Many women were confined in marriages of mutual convenience, happy to bury themselves in active social existences as their husbands' hostesses, in return for the trappings of success: the jewellery, exotic luxury cars, trips abroad.

Carly knew she'd trade it all willingly to erase the past seven years, to go back magically in time to the days when *love* was an irrepressible joy.

Now it was an empty shell, their sexual coupling merely an expression of physical lust untouched by any emotion from the heart.

Perhaps she was too honest, with too much personal integrity to survive within the constraints of such a marriage. Yet she was trapped, impossibly bound to Stefano by Ann-Marie. To remove her daughter from her father and return to their former existence would cause emotional scarring of such magnitude that the end result would be worthless.

'If you continue much longer, you'll end up with a headache.'

Carly's hand stilled at the sound of that deep drawling voice, and she stood motionless as Stefano moved to stand behind her.

'I have nothing to say to you,' she managed in stilted tones, watching him warily.

He was close, much too close for her peace of mind, and all her fine body hairs quivered in anticipation of his touch.

'We seem to manage very well without words,' he said with a degree of irony, and she lashed out verbally at his implication.

'Sex isn't the answer to everything, damn you!'

Her eyes unconsciously met his in the mirror, large and impossibly dark as she took in the image her body projected against the backdrop of his own.

Without the benefit of shoes, the tip of her head was level with his throat, and his breadth of shoulder had a dwarfing effect, making her appear small and incredibly vulnerable.

'No?' he queried softly, and she was damningly aware of the subtle pull of her senses as she fought his irresistible magnetism.

Her gaze remained locked with his, their darkness magnifying as he slowly lifted a hand and swept a heavy swath of her hair aside, baring the edge of her neck. His head slowly lowered as his mouth sought the pulsing cord in that sensitive curve, and she was powerless to prevent the sweet spiralling sensation that coursed through her body at his touch.

Carly was conscious of his hands as they shifted to her shoulders, then slid slowly down her arms to rest at her waist, before slipping up to cup the swollen fullness of her breasts.

She wanted to close her eyes and pretend the seduction was real, and for a few minutes she succumbed to temptation.

His fingers created a tactile magic, sensitising the engorged peaks until she moved restlessly against him, craving more than this subtle pleasuring. A hollow groan whispered from her throat as his hands slid to her shoulders, slipping the thin strap of her nightgown down over her arms, so that the thin silk slithered in a heap at her feet.

He didn't move, and she slowly opened her eyes to focus reluctantly on their mirrored image watching in mesmerised fascination as his hands slid round her waist and pressed her back against him.

Her eyes widened as she watched the effect he had on the texture of her skin, the tightening of her breasts, each tumescent peak aroused in anticipation of his possession.

It was almost as if he was forcing her to recognise something her conscious mind refused to acknowledge, and she gazed in mesmeric wonder as her body reacted to the light brush of his fingers as he trailed them across the curve of her waist, then slid to trace the soft mound of her stomach before allowing his fingers to splay into the soft curls protecting the central core of her femininity.

Of their own volition, her lower limbs swayed into the curve of his hand as they sought closer contact, and she was totally unprepared for the soft dreaminess evident in her eyes, the faint sheen on her parted lips.

She looked ... incandescently bewitched, held in thrall by passionate desire, and in that moment she felt she hated him for making her see a side of herself she preferred to keep well-hidden. Especially from him.

Yet it was too late, and even as she arched away he turned her fully into his arms, his mouth successfully covering hers in a manner that left her no hope of uttering so much as a word.

Her initial struggle was merely a token gesture, as was her determination to prevent his open-mouthed kiss. Seconds later she cried out as one long arm curved down the length of her back in a seeking quest for the tell-tale dewing at the aroused nub of her femininity.

Every nerve in her body seemed acutely sensitised, the internal tissues still faintly bruised from the previous night's loving, so much so that she tensed involuntarily against his touch.

Without a word he placed an arm beneath her knees and lifted her high against his chest to carry her to his bed, sinking down on to the mattress in one fluid movement as he cradled her gently into the curve of his body.

His lips trailed a path to her mouth, soothing her slight protest, before tracing a path down her neck. Slowly, with infinite care, he traversed each pleasure pulse, anointing the tender peak of each breast with delicate eroticism.

Her stomach quivered in betrayal beneath the seductive passage of his mouth, and when he reached the junction between her thighs she gave a beseeching moan, an entreaty to end the consuming madness that flared through her body, igniting it with flame.

Carly consoled herself that nothing mattered except this wonderful slaking of sensual pleasure in a slow, gentle loving that touched her soul. But in her subconscious mind she knew she lied, and she drifted into sleep wondering if there could ever be a resolution between the dictates of her brain and the wayward path of her emotions.

CHAPTER NINE

'I HAVE to attend a meeting on the Central Coast,' Stefano declared as he rose from the breakfast table. 'I doubt I'll be home before seven.'

'Angelica is naturally one of the associates accompanying you.' It wasn't a question, and he shot her a dark encompassing glance.

'She is on the board of a number of family companies,' he informed coolly. 'And a dedicated businesswoman.'

'Very dedicated,' Carly mocked, and was unable to resist adding, 'Have fun.'

After he left she finished her coffee, then moved quickly upstairs to change into a white cotton button-through dress, slipped her feet into flat sandals, then collected the keys to the BMW, informed Sylvana she'd be home in the late afternoon, and drove into the city.

There were a few things she wanted to pick up for Ann-Marie, and she'd fill in time between hospital visits by browsing the shops in the hope of gaining some inspiration for Christmas gifts.

Carly returned home at five, and after a leisurely shower she changed into a cool sage-green silk shift, wound her hair up into a casually contrived knot, then went downstairs to check on dinner with Sylvana.

The portable television was on in the kitchen, and highlighted on the screen was an area of dense bush-covered gorge and a hovering rescue helicopter. The presenter's modulated voice was relaying information regarding a light plane crash just south of the Central Coast. There were no survivors, and names had not yet been released of the pilot and two passengers.

Carly went cold. It was as if her limbs were frozen, for she couldn't move, and she gazed sightlessly at the flashing screen without comprehending a single thing.

Then she began to shake, and she clutched her arms together in an effort to contain her trembling limbs.

It couldn't be the plane carrying Stefano and Angelica—*could it*? A silent agonised scream rose in her throat. Dear God—*no*.

The thought of his strong body lying broken and burned in dense undergrowth almost destroyed her. His image was a vivid entity, and she saw his strongly etched features, the dark gleaming eyes, almost as if he were in the same room.

The phone rang, but the sound barely registered, nor did Sylvana's voice as she answered the call, until it seemed to change in tone and Carly realised that Sylvana was attempting to gain her attention.

'Stefano rang to say he'll be home in twenty minutes.'

The words penetrated her brain, barely registering in those initial few seconds, then she turned slowly, her eyes impossibly large. 'What did you say?'

Sylvana repeated the message, then added in puzzlement, 'Are you all right?'

Carly inclined her head, then murmured some-thing indistinguishable as her stomach began to churn, and she only just made it upstairs to the main suite before she was violently ill.

Afterwards she clenched her teeth, then she sluiced warm water over her face in an effort to dispel the chilled feeling that seemed to invade her bones.

Attempting to repair the ravages with make-up moved her to despair, for she looked incredibly vulnerable—*haunted*, she amended silently as she examined her mirrored image with critical deliberation.

How could you *love* someone you professed to hate? Yet an inner voice taunted that love and hate were intense emotions and closely entwined. Legend had it that they were inseparable.

Stefano's arrival home was afforded a restrained greeting. If she'd listened to her heart she would have flown into his arms and expressed a profound relief that he was alive. Yet then he couldn't fail to be aware of her true feelings, and that would never do.

Consequently dinner was strained, and Carly failed to do any justice to Sylvana's beautifully pre-pared food, and throughout the meal she was con-scious of his veiled scrutiny, so much so that she felt close to screaming with angry vexation.

'Did it bother you that it might have been my body lying lifeless in some rocky gorge?'

The blood drained from her face at his drawled query, and she got to her feet, wanting only to get away from his ill-disguised mockery.

She hadn't moved more than two paces when hard hands closed over her shoulders, and she struggled in vain, hot, angry tears clouding her eyes as she fought to be free of him.

One hand slid to hold her nape fast, tilting her head, and her lashes swept down to form a protective veil, only to fly open as his mouth closed over hers in a hard open-mouthed kiss that was impossibly, erotically demanding.

It seemed to go on forever, and when it was over she lifted shaking fingers to her lips.

His eyes were dark with brooding savagery, their depths filled with latent passion and an emotion she didn't even attempt to define. Carly glanced past him and fixed her eyes on a distant wall in an attempt to regain her composure. If she looked at him she knew she'd disgrace herself with stupid ignominious tears.

'I rang through the instant we touched base,' he enlightened quietly. 'Our helicopter pilot sighted the crash, radioed for help, then circled the area until a rescue unit arrived.' He raised a hand and trailed gentle fingers along the edge of her cheek.

She lifted her shoulders in a faint shrugging gesture. Somehow she had to inject an element of normality, otherwise she was doomed. 'Would you like some coffee?'

A forefinger probed the softness of her swollen lower lip, then conducted a leisurely tracery of its outline. 'I'd like *you*,' Stefano drawled in mocking tones, and watched the expressive play of emotions chase each other across her mobile features.

'It's early,' she stalled, hating the way her body was reacting to the proximity of his.

'Since when did time have anything to do with making love?' His head lowered and he touched his mouth to the thudding pulse at the edge of her neck, then traced a path to her temple. His lips pressed closed one eyelid, then the other, and his hands shifted as he caught her up in his arms.

'What are you doing?' The cry was torn from her lips as he calmly strode from the room, and headed for the stairs.

'Taking you to bed,' Stefano declared in a husky undertone, 'in an attempt to remove the look of shadowed anguish lurking in your beautiful eyes.'

She struggled in helplessness against him, aware of an elemental quality that was infinitely awesome. No one man deserved so much power, or quite such a degree of latent sensuality.

'Must you be so—physical?' she protested as he entered their suite and closed the door.

He lowered her down to stand within the circle of his arms, and her limbs seemed weightless as he caught her close. Then he kissed her, slowly and with such evocative mastery that she didn't have the energy to voice any further protest as he carefully removed her clothes, then released the pins holding her hair before beginning on his own.

'Tell me to stop,' he murmured seconds before his mouth closed over hers, and the flame that burned deep within them flared into vibrant life, consuming them both in a passionate storm that lasted far into the night.

The following days settled into a relatively normal routine. The nights were something else as Carly fought a silent battle with herself and invariably lost.

Their lovemaking scaled hitherto unreached heights, transcending mere pleasure, and it was almost as if some inner song were demanding to be heard, yet the music was indistinct, the words just beyond her reach.

Introspection became an increasing trap in which she found herself caught, in the insidious recognition that *love* was inextricably interwoven with physical desire—which inevitably led to the agonising question of Angelica, and the degree of Stefano's personal involvement. Were they still on intimate terms? *Had they ever been*? Dear God, could she have been wrong all these years?

One day in particular she couldn't bear the tension any more, and she moved restlessly through the house, unsure how to fill the few hours until it was time to visit Ann-Marie.

Making a split-second decision, she changed clothes, stroked a clear gloss over her lips, then caught up her sunglasses and bag, and made her way down to the car, intent on spending a few more hours in the city looking for suitable Christmas gifts. She might even do lunch.

Two hours later Carly wasn't sure shopping was such a good idea. It was hot, there were crowds of people all intent on doing the same thing, and it took ages to be served. All she'd achieved was a bottle of Sarah's favourite French perfume, a book and an educational game for Ann-Marie, and nothing for Stefano. What did you buy a man who had everything? she queried with scepticism. Another silk tie? A silk shirt? Something as mundane as *aftershave*, when she didn't even recognise what brand he preferred?

A glance at her watch revealed that it was after one. Something to eat and a cool drink would provide a welcome break, and ten minutes later she was seated in a pleasant air-conditioned restaurant eating a succulent chicken salad.

'Mind if I join you?'

Carly glanced up and endeavoured to contain her surprise. Coincidence was a fine thing, and the chance of choosing the same restaurant as Angelica Agnelli had to run at a thousand to one. 'If you must,' she responded with bare civility. The restaurant *was* crowded, after all, and short of being rude there wasn't much she could do except accept the situation with as much grace as possible.

'Shopping?' Angelica queried, arching an elegantly shaped eyebrow as she caught sight of the brightly designed bags.

'Yes.' As if an explanation was needed, she added, 'Christmas.'

'Stefano is caught up in a conference, so I came on ahead.' She allowed the information to sink in, then added with deadly timing, 'This is a charmingly secluded place, don't you agree?' For furtive assignations. The implication was there for anyone but the most obtuse, but just in case there was any doubt she added smoothly, 'You don't normally lunch here, do you?'

'No. I preferred to eat a packed lunch at my desk,' Carly explained with considerable calm, and tempered the words with a seemingly sweet smile.

Angelica deliberately allowed her eyes to widen. 'Rather clever of you to present Stefano with a child conveniently the right age to be his own.' Her mouth curled fractionally. 'I almost advised him to insist on a DNA test.' She lifted a hand and appeared to study her immaculately manicured nails. 'But of course, I wouldn't presume to interfere in his...' She trailed off deliberately, then added with barbed innuendo, 'Private affairs.'

'You've obviously changed your strategy,' Carly returned with considerable fortitude, when inside she felt like screaming.

'Whatever do you mean?'

Carly had quite suddenly had enough. 'You had no such compunction about interfering in his private life seven years ago. You deliberately set out to destroy me. Like a fool, I ran.' Her eyes sparked gold-flecked fire that caused the other woman's expression to narrow. 'I realise your association with Stefano goes back a long time, but perhaps you should understand it was *he* who did the chasing in our relationship, and he who insisted on a reconciliation.' She drew in a deep breath, then released it slowly. 'Stefano has had seven years to instigate divorce proceedings.' Her voice assumed a quietly fierce intensity. 'I would suggest you ask yourself why he never did.'

'*Brava*,' a deep voice drawled quietly from behind, and Carly closed her eyes in vexation, only to open them again.

Stefano stood indolently at ease, his expression strangely watchful as he took in Carly's pale features. All of her pent-up emotion was visible in the expressive brilliance of her eyes, their gold-flecked depths ringed in black.

'Stefano.' Angelica's tone held a conciliatory purr, yet his eyes never moved from Carly's features.

'If you'll excuse me?' She had to get out of here before she erupted with volatile rage—with Angelica for being a bitch, and Stefano simply because he was *here*.

Rising to her feet, she collected her bag and assorted carriers. 'Enjoy your lunch.'

His hand closed on her arm, bringing her to a halt, and she just looked at him, then her lashes swept down in a bid to hide the pain that gnawed deep inside.

'Please. Let me go.' Her voice was softly pitched, yet filled with aching intensity, and there was nothing she could do to prevent the descent of his mouth or the brief, hard open-mouthed kiss he bestowed.

Then he released her, and it took all her reserve of strength to walk calmly from the restaurant.

By the time she reached the street her lips were quivering with pent-up emotion, and she fumbled for her sunglasses, glad of their protective lenses as they hid the well of tears that blurred her vision.

Tonight there would be no respite, for Sarah and James were coming to dinner. To present anything approaching a normal façade would take every ounce of acting ability, and Carly wished fervently for the day to be done, and the night.

Only a matter of weeks ago everything had seemed so uncomplicated. Ann-Marie and work had been the total focus of her life. Now she was in turmoil, her emotions as wild and uncontrollable as a storm-tossed sea.

At the hospital, Ann-Marie's exuberant greeting, the loving hug and beautiful smile acted to diffuse Carly's inner tension, and she listened to her daughter's excited chatter about a new patient who had been admitted that morning.

As Carly left the hospital and drove home she couldn't help wishing her life were clear-cut, and there were no tensions, no subtle game-playing that ate at the heartstrings and destroyed one's self-esteem.

Perhaps she should stop fighting this conflict within herself and just accept the status quo, be content with her existence as Stefano's wife, and condone the pleasure they shared each night. To hunger for anything more was madness.

After garaging the car, Carly consulted with Sylvana, made suitably appreciative comments, then opted to cool off with a leisurely swim in the pool.

Stefano arrived home as Carly was putting the finishing touches to her make-up, and she turned as he entered their suite, her expression deliberately bland as she registered his tall, dark-suited frame before lifting her head to meet his gaze.

His eyes were dark, probing hers, and after a fleeting glance her own skittered towards the vicinity of his left shoulder. The last thing she needed was a confrontation. Not with Sarah and James due within minutes.

'I'll go down and check with Sylvana,' Carly said evenly. 'I'll wait for you in the lounge.'

It was a relief to escape his presence, and she was grateful for Sarah's punctuality, immensely glad of her friend's warm personality.

The meal was a gourmet's delight, and although
onversation flowed with ease Carly merely oper-
ted on automatic pilot as she forked food inter-
ittently into her mouth, then toyed with the
emainder on her plate.

She laughed, genuinely enjoying Sarah's anec-
otes intermingled with those of James, but all the
hile she felt like a disembodied spectator.

It was almost ten when they rose from the table.

'I'll make the coffee,' Carly declared, and smiled
hen Sarah rose to her feet.

'I'll help you.'

Sylvana had set everything ready in the kitchen,
 that all Carly had to do was percolate the coffee.

'How are things going——?' Carly broke off with
 laugh in the realisation that Sarah was asking the
me question simultaneously with her own. 'You
 first,' she bade her, shooting her friend a smiling
ance.

'Where shall I start?' Sarah returned with a grin
; she crossed to the servery, and cast the stylish
tchen an appreciative glance. 'Lucky you,' she
niled without a trace of envy. 'All this, and
efano, too.'

'Sarah...' Carly warned with a low growl, and
arah grinned unrepentantly.

'James and Stefano seem to have a lot in
mmon,' Sarah offered innocuously, her eyes
arkling as Carly shot her a speaking glance.
ames is nice,' she admitted quietly. 'I like him.'

'And?' Carly prompted.

'Sometimes I think I could get used to the idea
 a relationship with him, then I'm not sure I want
 make that sort of change to my life.' Her eyes

sought Carly's, and her voice softened. 'How abou
you?'

'Ann-Marie is improving daily.'

'That wasn't what I asked,' Sarah admonishe
teasingly, and Carly's expression became faint
pensive.

'I seem to swing like a pendulum between resen
ment and acceptance.'

'You look . . .' Sarah paused, her eyes narrowir
with thoughtful speculation. 'Pregnant. Are you

Carly opened her mouth to deny it, then close
it again as her mind rapidly calculated dates. H
eyes became an expressive host to a number of
varying fleeting emotions.

'You have that certain look a woman possess
in the initial few weeks,' Sarah observed gently. '
subtle tiredness as the body refocuses its energ
You had the same look the day we met moving in
neighbouring apartments,' she added softly.

'It could be stress from juggling twice-daily ho
pital visits, marriage,' Carly offered in strangle
tones as the implications of a possible pregnan
began to sink in. She *couldn't* be, surely? Yet t
symptoms were all there, added to facts she'd be
too busy to notice.

She lifted a shaking hand, then let it fall agai
and for one heartfelt second her eyes filled wi
naked pain before she successfully masked the
expression.

'The coffee is perking,' Sarah reminded gent
and Carly crossed to turn down the heat, then wh
it was ready she placed it on the tray.

The men were deep in conversation when Ca
and Sarah re-entered the lounge, and if either o

ected that the girls' smiles were a little too bright hey gave no sign.

It was almost eleven when Sarah indicated the need to leave, explaining, 'I'm due to go on duty tomorrow morning at seven.' She rose to her feet, thanked both Stefano and Carly for a delightful evening, and at the door she gave Carly a quick hug in farewell. 'Ring me when you can.'

Carly turned back towards the lobby the instant the car headlights disappeared down the drive, moving into the lounge to collect coffee-cups together prior to carrying them through to the kitchen.

'Leave them,' Stefano instructed as he saw what he was doing. 'Sylvana can take care of it in the morning.'

'It will only take a minute.' In the kitchen, she rinsed and stacked them in the dishwasher, then turned to find him leaning against the edge of the table, watching her with narrowed scrutiny.

She stood perfectly still, despite every nerve-end screaming at fever pitch, and her chin lifted fractionally as he took the necessary steps towards her.

'What now, Stefano?' Carly queried with a touch of defiance. 'A post-mortem on lunch?'

One eyebrow slanted in mocking query. 'What part of lunch would you particularly like to refer to?'

'I disliked being publicly labelled as your possession,' she insisted, stung by his cynicism.

'Yet you are,' he declared silkily. 'My feelings where you're concerned verge on the primitive.'

A tiny pulse quickened at the base of her throat, then began to hammer in palpable confusion as she

absorbed the essence of his words. 'Is that meant
to frighten me?'

Tension filled the air, lending a highly volatile
quality that was impossible to ignore. 'Only if you
choose to allow it,' he mocked, and she stood perfectly still as he conducted a slow, all-encompassing
appraisal, lingering on the deepness of her eyes, and
her soft, trembling mouth.

He lifted a hand to brush gentle fingers across
her cheek, and she reared back as if from a lick of
flame.

'Don't touch me.'

'Whyever not, *cara*?'

'Because that's where it starts and ends,' she as-
serted with a mixture of despair and wretchedness.

'You find my lovemaking so distasteful?'

His musing indulgence was the living end, and
she lashed out at him with expressive anger. '*Lust*,
damn you!' she corrected heatedly, so incensed that
she balled both hands into fists and punched him,
uncaring that she connected with the hard, muscular wall of his chest.

'Lust is a bartered commodity. What would you
like me to give you?' His voice was a low-pitched
drawl that cut right through to the heart. 'An item
of jewellery, perhaps?'

For several long seconds she just looked at him,
filled with an aching pain so acute that it took all
her effort to breathe evenly. What was the use, she
agonised silently, of aiming for something that
didn't exist?

'In return for which I reward you in bed?' The
words were out before she had time to give them

much thought, and afterwards it was too late to retract them.

His dark brooding glance narrowed fractionally, then his mouth curved in mocking amusement. 'Ah, *cara*,' he taunted softly. 'You reward me so well.'

The need to get away from him, even temporarily, was paramount, and she turned towards the door, only to be brought to a halt as hard hands caught hold of each shoulder and spun her round.

Her eyes blazed with anger through a mist of tears as she tilted her head in silent apathy, hating him more at that precise moment than she thought it possible to hate anyone.

'Stop making fun of me! I won't have it, do you hear?' Angry, frustrated tears filled her eyes as he restrained her with galling ease, and she shook her head helplessly as he drew her inextricably close.

'*Don't*——' Carly begged, feeling the familiar pull of her senses. It would be so easy to succumb, simply to close her eyes and become transported by the special magic of their shared sexual alchemy.

'When have I ever made fun of you?' he teased gently, and she shivered slightly as one hand slid down over the soft roundness of her bottom, pressing her close against the unmistakable force of his arousal, while the other slid up to cup her nape.

'Every time I oppose you,' she began shakily, then, gathering the scattered threads of her courage, she continued with strengthened resolve. 'You resolve it by sweeeping me off to bed.' Lifting her hands, she attempted to put some distance between them, only to fail miserably.

'Am I to be damned forever for finding you
desirable?'

The thread of amusement in his voice hurt unbearably. 'I'm not a sex object you can use merely
to satisfy a need for revenge.'

His eyes searched hers, dark and unfathomable
as he held her immobile.

'Let me go, damn you!'

He looked at her in silence for what seemed an
age, his eyes darkening until they resembled the
deepest slate—hard and equally obdurate.

'Does it feel like revenge every time I take you
in my arms?' he queried with dangerous silkiness.

It was heaven and the entire universe rolled into
one, ecstasy at its zenith. She looked at him for
what seemed an age, unable to utter so much as a
word.

Dared she take the chance? All the pent-up anger
her so-called resentment, dissipated as if it had
never existed.

'No,' Carly voiced quietly, and he shook her
gently, sliding his hands from her shoulders up to
cup her face.

'From the moment I first met you I wanted to
lock you in a gilded prison and throw away the key.
Except such a primitive action wouldn't have been
condoned in this day and age.' His eyes were level
and she was unable to drag her own away from the
darkness or the pain evident. 'You were a prime
target . . . young, and incredibly susceptible,' he enlightened her softly.

'If I had been able to get my hands on you during
those first few weeks after you left Perth I think
would have strangled you,' he continued slowly.

'Your mother disavowed any knowledge of your whereabouts, and I soon realised you had no intention of contacting me.' His voice hardened measurably, and assumed a degree of cynicism. 'The letter dispatched from your solicitor merely confirmed it.'

He was silent for so long that she wondered if he intended to continue.

'A marriage has no foundation without trust, and as you professed to have lost your trust in me I let you go. Fully expecting,' he added with a trace of mockery, 'to be officially notified of an impending divorce.'

He hadn't been able to instigate such proceedings any more than she had. Her heart set up a quickened beat.

'Not long after shifting base to Sydney I attended an accounting seminar with a fellow associate at which Clive Mathorpe was a guest speaker. I was impressed. Sufficiently so to utilise his services.' He proffered a faint smile. 'Coincidence, *fate* perhaps, that Carly Taylor *Alessi* should be a respected member of his firm. The night I met you at Clive's home I was intrigued by your maturity and self-determination. And very much aware that the intense sexual magic we once shared was still in evidence.' His eyes held hers, and his voice was deliberate as he continued, 'For both of us.'

Carly looked at him carefully, seeing his innate strength, the power in evidence, and knew that she would never willingly want to be apart from him. It was always easy, with hindsight, to rationalise—to indulge in a series of 'what if's, and 'if only's. Maturity had taught her there could only be *now*.

'Angelica's ammunition was pretty powerful,' she offered quietly. 'I found it emotionally damaging at the time.'

There was a mesmeric silence, intensifying until she became conscious of every breath she took.

'I have known Angelica from birth,' Stefano revealed with deceptive mildness, and a muscle tensed along the edge of his jaw. 'Our affiliation owes itself to two sets of parents who immigrated to Australia more than forty years ago. They prospered in one business venture after another, achieving phenomenal success. So much so that hope was fostered that the only Alessi son might marry an Agnelli daughter and thus form a dynasty.' He paused fractionally, and searched her pale features, seeing the faint shadows evident beneath her eyes. 'It was a game I chose not to play,' he added gently.

Carly swallowed the lump that had suddenly risen in her throat. 'The way Angelica told it,' she informed him shakily, 'you were unofficially betrothed when you met me. If our engagement surprised her, our wedding threw her into a rage,' she continued, unwilling to expound too graphically on just how much she'd been hurt by a woman who refused to face reality. 'It appeared I was merely a temporary diversion, and there was little doubt she intended to be there to pick up the pieces.' She effected a deprecatory shrug that hid a measure of pain.

'Angelica,' Stefano declared hardly, 'possesses a vivid imagination. After today,' he grained out with chilling inflexibility, 'she has no doubt whom I love or why.' His expression softened as he watched the expressive play of emotions chasing each other

across her features. '*You*, Carly,' he elaborated
gently. 'Always. Only you.'

Stefano shifted his hold, catching both her hands
together in one of his, feeling her body quiver
slightly as he traced a gentle pattern over the slim
curve of her stomach before resting possessively at
her trim waist. When his gaze met hers, she nearly
died at the lambent warmth revealed in those dark
depths.

'There is nothing else you want to tell me?'

Carly stood hesitantly unsure, and at the last
moment courage failed her. Slowly she shook her
head.

Tomorrow, she'd visit the doctor and undergo a
pregnancy test. Then she'd tell him.

CHAPTER TEN

THE morning began the same as any other week day. Stefano rose early, swam several lengths of the pool, ate breakfast with his wife, then showered, dressed and left for the city.

At nine Carly checked with Sylvana, then changed into a smart lemon-yellow button-through linen dress, applied make-up with care, slid her feet into elegant shoes, and went downstairs to the car.

The pregnancy test was performed with ease, and pronounced positive. Carly drove on to the hospital in a state of suspended euphoria.

Ann-Marie looked really *well*, her eyes bright and shining as Carly walked into her room, and her beautiful hair was beginning to show signs of growth. A consultation with the specialist revealed that Ann-Marie could be discharged the following day.

Carly almost floated down the carpeted corridor, and on impulse she crossed to the pay-phone, checked the directory, slotted in coins and keyed in the appropriate series of digits, then relayed specific instructions to the voice on the other end of the phone.

A small secretive smile tugged the edges of her mouth as she drove into the city, and twenty minutes later she stood completing formalities in Reception at one of the inner city's most elegant hotels.

The lift whisked her with swift precision to the eleventh floor, and inside the luxurious suite she swiftly crossed the room, lifted the handset and dialled a memorised number.

She was mad, absolutely crazy, she derided as the line engaged after a number of electronic beeps. What if Stefano wasn't in the office? Worse, what if he was in an important meeting, and couldn't leave? she agonised as the number connected with his personal mobile net.

'Alessi.' His voice sounded brisk and impersonal, and her stomach flipped, then executed a number of painful somersaults.

'Stefano.'

'Carly. Is something wrong?'

'No——' *Hell*, she was faltering, stammering like a schoolgirl. Taking a deep breath, she clenched the receiver and forced herself to speak calmly. 'I'm fine.' Dammit, this was proving more difficult than she'd envisaged.

'Ann-Marie?'

'She's coming home tomorrow.' The joy in her voice was a palpable entity that was reciprocated in his.

Do it, *tell* him, a tiny voice prompted. 'I wanted to ring and say...' She hesitated slightly, then uttered the words with slow emphasis. '*I love you.*'

A few seconds of silence followed, then his voice sounded incredibly husky close to her ear. 'Where are you?'

'In a hotel room, in the city.'

His soft laughter sent spirals of sensation shooting through her body. 'Which hotel, *cara*?'

She named it. 'It's Sylvana's day to vacuum,' she explained a trifle breathlessly.

'Ensuring that total privacy is out of the question,' he drawled with a tinge of humour.

'Totally,' she agreed, and a tiny smile teased the edges of her mouth. 'Is this a terribly inconvenient time for you?'

'It wouldn't make any difference.'

Her heart leapt, then began thudding to a quickened beat. 'No?'

His husky chuckle did strange things to her equilibrium. 'I'll be with you in twenty minutes.'

Carly relayed the room number, then softly replaced the receiver.

Twenty minutes, she mused as she eased off her shoes. How could she fill them? Make a cup of coffee, perhaps, or select a chilled mineral water from the variety stocked in the bar-fridge.

Her eyes travelled idly round the large room, noting the customary prints, the wall-lights, before settling on the bed.

If she turned down the covers, it would look too blatant, and she didn't quite possess the courage to remove all her clothes. What if she opened the door to find a maid or steward on the other side? she thought wildly.

Damn. Waiting was agony, and she crossed to the sealed window and stood watching the traffic on the busy street below.

Everyone appeared to be hurrying, and when the southbound traffic ground to a halt a clutch of people surged across the road to the opposite side. The lights turned green, and the northbound traffic gathered momentum, moving in a seemingly endless river of vehicles until green changed to amber and then to red, when the process began all over again.

From this height everything seemed lilliputian, and she watched the cars, searching for the sleek lines of Stefano's top-of-the-range Mercedes, although the likelihood of catching sight of it when she wasn't even sure from which direction he'd be travelling seemed remote.

It was a beautiful day, she perceived idly. There was a cloudless sky of azure-blue, the sun filtering in shafts of brilliant light between the tall city buildings.

Time became a suspended entity, and it seemed an age before she heard the quiet double knock at the door.

Her stomach reacted at once, leaping almost into her throat, and she smoothed suddenly damp hands down the seams of her dress as she crossed the suite to open the door.

Stefano stood at ease, his tall frame filling the aperture, and she simply looked at him in silence. There was a vital, almost electric energy apparent, an inherent vitality that was compelling, and her pulse accelerated into a rapid beat.

A faint smile teased his generous mouth, and his eyes were so incredibly warm that she almost melted beneath their gaze.

'Do you intend to keep me standing here?'

Pale pink tinged her cheeks as she stood to one side. Fool, she berated herself silently, feeling about as composed as a lovestruck teenager as she followed him into the centre of the room.

When he turned she was within touching distance, yet he made no attempt to draw her into his arms.

'I gather there was a degree of urgency in the need to book in to a hotel room?'

There was no mistaking his soft teasing drawl, nor the expression evident in his eyes. It gave her the confidence to resort to humour.

The sparkle in the depths of her eyes flared into brilliant life, and she laughed softly. 'Tonight we're supposed to dine out with Sarah and James to celebrate Sarah's birthday. If it were anyone else, I wouldn't hesitate to cancel.' A devilish gleam emerged, dancing in the light of her smile. 'I did consider a confrontation in your office, but the thought of Renate or any one of the staff catching sight of their exalted boss deep in an erotic clinch might prove too embarrassing to be condoned.'

His lips twitched, then settled into a sensual curve. 'Erotic?'

'There's champagne in the bar-fridge,' Carly announced inconsequentially. 'Would you like some?'

'I'd like you to repeat what you said to me on the phone,' he commanded gently, and her eyes were remarkably clear as they held his.

'I love you. I always have,' she stressed.

'*Grazie amore.*' He reached out and pulled her close in against him. His lips brushed her forehead, then began a slow, tantalising trail down to the edge of her mouth.

'You're my life,' he said huskily. 'My love.'

There was such a wealth of emotion in his voice; she felt a delicious warmth begin deep within her as a thousand tiny nerve-endings leapt into pulsating life.

'So many wasted years,' she offered with deep regret. 'Nights,' she elaborated huskily. 'Dear heaven, I *missed* you.'

Her eyes widened as she glimpsed the expression in those dark depths mere inches above her own, then she gasped as his mouth moved to cover hers in a kiss that left her feeling shaken with a depth of emotion so intoxicating that it was as if she was soaring high on to a sensual pinnacle of such incredible magnitude that she felt weightless, and totally malleable.

'*Don't*,' Stefano chastised softly. 'We have today, and all the tomorrows. A lifetime.'

Her eyes were wondrously expressive as she lifted her hands and wound them round his neck. 'What time do you have to be back at the office?'

'I told Renate to reschedule the remainder of the day's appointments,' he revealed solemnly.

A delightfully bewitching smile lit her features, and her lips curved to form a teasing smile. 'We have until two, when I visit Ann-Marie in hospital.'

His hands slid down over her hips, and she gloried in the feel of him as he drew her close and brushed his lips close to her ear. 'We'll go together.' The tip of his tongue traced the sensitive whorls, and she shivered as sensation shafted through her body.

A soft laugh bubbled up from her throat to emerge as an exultant sound of delicious anticipation. 'Meantime, I have a few plans for the next few hours.' Leaning away from him, she murmured her pleasure as he loosened his hold so that she could slip the jacket from his shoulders.

His eyes gleamed with humour, and a wealth of latent passion. 'Do you, indeed?'

'Uh-huh.' Her fingers set to work on his tie, then the buttons of his shirt. The belt buckle came next, and she hesitated fractionally as she undid the fastener at his waist and freed the zip. 'Something wildly imaginative with champagne and strawberries.' A bubble of laughter emerged from her throat. 'It's rather decadent.'

His shoes followed, his socks, until all he wore was a pair of silk briefs.

'My turn, I think.'

With unhurried movements he removed every last vestige of her clothing, then he leaned down and tugged back the covers from the large bed before gently pulling her down to lie beside him.

His kiss melted her bones, and she gasped as his mouth began a treacherous path of discovery that encompassed every inch, every vulnerable hollow of her body.

By the time his lips returned to caress hers, there wasn't one coherent word she was capable of uttering, and she clung to him, eager, wanting, *needing* the sweet savagery of his lovemaking.

A long time afterwards she lay catching her breath as she attempted to control the waywardness of her emotions, then slowly she moved, affording him a similar pleasuring until he groaned and pulled her to lie on top of him.

'Minx,' he growled softly, curving a hand round her nape and urging her mouth down to his. 'Keep doing that, and I won't be answerable for the consequences.'

'Promises, promises,' Carly taunted gently as she initiated a kiss that he allowed her to control. Then she rose up and arched her back, stretching like a kitten that had just had its fill of cream.

The soft sigh of contentment changed to a faint gasp as he positioned her to accept his length, and now it was he who was in command, watching her fleeting emotions with musing indulgence as he led her towards a climactic orgasmic explosion that had her crying out his name as wave after wave of sensation exploded from deep within her feminine core, radiating to the furthest reaches of her body in an all-consuming pleasurable ache that gradually ebbed to a warm afterglow, lasting long after they'd shared a leisurely shower and slipped into the complimentary towelling robes.

'Hmm,' Carly murmured as Stefano came to stand behind her and drew her back into the circle of his arms. 'I'm hungry.' She felt his lips caress her nape, and she turned slightly towards him. 'For food, you insatiable man!'

'Do you want to dress and go down to the restaurant, or shall I order Room Service?'

She pretended to consider both options, then directed him a teasing smile. 'Room Service.' She was loath to share him with anyone, and although the time was fast approaching when they must dress and leave she wanted to delay it as long as possible. 'Besides,' she teased mercilessly, 'there's still the champagne.'

Choosing from the menu and placing their order took only minutes, and afterwards Stefano pulled her back into his arms and held her close.

She drew in a deep breath, then released it slowly 'I've been giving some thought to going back t work next year.'

His eyes took on a new depth, then assumed musing speculative gleam. 'What if I were to mak you a better offer?'

'Such as?'

'Working from home, maintaining order with m paperwork, liaising with Renate?'

Carly pretended to consider his proposal, tiltin her head to one side in silent contemplation.

'Flexible hours, harmonious working cor ditions, and intimate terms with the boss?' sb teased.

'Very intimate terms,' he conceded with a slopin smile.

'I accept. Conditionally,' she added with a tempted solemnity, and was unable to prevent th slight catch in her breath. 'I'm not sure of you stance on employing pregnant women.'

He didn't say anything for a few seconds, the he kissed her, so gently and with such reverenc that it was all she could do not to cry.

'Thank you,' Stefano said simply, and she smile a trifle tremulously.

'If this pregnancy follows the same pattern as did with Ann-Marie,' she warned with musing r flection, 'I'll begin feeling nauseous within the ne few weeks.' She wrinkled her nose at him in siler humour. 'How will you cope with a wife who h to leap out of bed and run to the bathroom ever morning?'

'Ensure that you have whatever it is you nee until such time as you feel you can face the day.

Carly blinked rapidly, then offered shakily, 'Did I tell you how much I love you?'

Room Service delivered their lunch, but it was another hour before they ate the food. Afterwards they slowly dressed and made their way down to the car park.

'I'll follow you to the hospital,' Stefano said gently as he saw her seated behind the wheel of her car. 'Travel carefully, *cara*.'

'We really should stop meeting like this,' Carly declared with impish humour, and heard his husky laugh. Her smile widened into something so beautiful that he caught his breath. 'People might get the wrong idea,' she said with mock-solemnity.

'Indeed?'

'Indeed,' she concurred with a bewitching smile. 'I think we should limit it to special occasions.'

'Such as?'

She fastened her seatbelt, then fired the engine. 'Oh, I'm sure I'll think of something.' With a devilish grin, she engaged the gear, then eased the car out of its parking bay. '*Ciao, caro.*'

She felt deliciously wicked as she cleared the exit and slid into the flow of traffic. An exultant laugh emerged from her throat.

Anyone could be forgiven for thinking she was a mistress having an affair with a passionate lover. And she was. Except that the lover was her husband, and there was nothing illicit or furtive about their relationship.

Only mutual love and a shared bond that would last a lifetime.

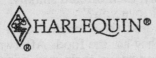 **HARLEQUIN®**

The proprietors of Weddings, Inc. hope you have enjoyed visiting Eternity, Massachusetts. And if you missed any of the exciting Weddings, Inc. titles, here is your opportunity to complete your collection:

HARLEQUIN
PRESENTS Plus

When Prince Uzziah invited Beth back to his sumptuous palace, she thought he was about to sell her the Arab stallion of her dreams. But Uzziah had another deal on his mind—a race...where the winner took all....

Kelda had always clashed with her stepbrother, Angelo, but now he was interfering in her life. He claimed it was for family reasons, and he demanded Kelda enter into a new relationship with him—as his mistress!

What would you do if *you* were Beth or Kelda? Share their pleasure and their passion—watch for:

Beth and the Barbarian by Miranda Lee
Harlequin Presents Plus #1711

and

Angel of Darkness by Lynne Graham
Harlequin Presents Plus #1712

Harlequin Presents Plus
The best has just gotten better!

Available in January wherever Harlequin books are sold.

This holiday, join four hunky heroes under the mistletoe for

Christmas Kisses

Cuddle under a fluffy quilt, with a cup of hot chocolate and these romances sure to warm you up:

#561 HE'S A REBEL (also a Studs title)
Linda Randall Wisdom

#562 THE BABY AND THE BODYGUARD
Jule McBride

#563 THE GIFT-WRAPPED GROOM
M.J. Rodgers

#564 A TIMELESS CHRISTMAS
Pat Chandler

Celebrate the season with all four holiday books sealed with a Christmas kiss—coming to you in December, only from Harlequin American Romance!

CHRISTMAS STALKINGS

All wrapped up in spine-tingling packages, here are three books guaranteed to chill your spine...and warm your hearts this holiday season!

#302 THE KID WHO STOLE CHRISTMAS
Linda Stevens

#303 I'LL BE HOME FOR CHRISTMAS
Dawn Stewardson

#304 BEARING GIFTS
Aimée Thurlo

This December, fill your stockings with the "Christmas Stalkings"—for the best in romantic suspense. Only from

HARLEQUIN®

INTRIGUE®

HARLEQUIN ◆ PRESENTS®

It may be winter—but the heat is on!

Watch out for
stories that will get your temperature rising...

they're

Watch for:

Southern Passions by Sara Wood
Harlequin Presents #1715

When Ros returned to New Orleans, Chance dismissed her
as another old flame out to snare him after his divorce. Still
there was an undeniable attraction, and passion simmered in
the steamy summer nights—until Chance discovered that
Ros wasn't after him at all....

Available in January wherever Harlequin books are sold.